# THE BEST
# AUSTRALIAN
# STORIES
# 2 0 0 4

# THE BEST
# AUSTRALIAN
# STORIES
## 2004

Edited by
FRANK MOORHOUSE

# Contents

# Memorandum from the Editor

## Frank Moorhouse

> The real fun of reading is in the re-reading.
> —Ben Fischer, graduate student, University of Texas

This year *Best Australian Stories* called for short stories written or published between 31 August 2003 and 1 September 2004, both from the writing community and from the public at large.

I felt gratified by the huge number of people – about 600 – who sent stories, and by the creative effort that the stories represent. I have read for competitions, for anthologies, and as an editor of magazines, and never before have I been exposed in such a short time to such fine writing and such intriguing and venturesome stories.

In this year's *Best Australian Stories* there is room for only twenty-seven stories. I could have confidently put together a book of fifty stories.

Of the stories selected, six were from first-time published writers. The youngest, Alli Barnard, is nineteen; the others are Nathan Besser, Bridget Brooklyn, Susan Coleridge, Jaimee Edwards and Tiffany Barton.

The stories submitted changed my thinking about the short story form. I was particularly interested in the innovations which are occurring within the form, especially in the freeing up of the visual design of the stories, which I suspect has been invited by the word processor although, admittedly, Laurence Sterne and James Joyce pioneered this. These innovations are in the *ordering* or lay-out of the story, the development of the notion of narrative *assembly*. The writers have found new ways of working with reader focus, of creating narrative tension and of managing the energy and movement of the story.

But I want to say that fine stories are also being written in the traditional formats and in the realist genre. And I am pleased to record that the great Australian motif of the banging screen door is still alive and well in the short story.

I believe that the contributors to this volume (and some of those I could not include) set a new benchmark in the standard of the short story.

In publicity before the call for submissions I expressed concern about the future of the literary short story. This fear came from the decline in the pathways to readership for the short story. But what the entries have revealed to me is that there is still a vibrant, if uneven, subculture of the short story. It lives on in dozens of small competitions, some local, some regional, some state-wide, run by writers' centres, by local government and by other organisations; at public readings; and in dozens of very small journals produced by writers' groups, by individuals and by schools of writing.

I still worry that the short story has become sub-economic, that is, that there is little economic validation afforded it and that, as an art form, it is not garnering sufficient resources from society to permit sustained serious work with the form.

Because the population of Australia is steadily increasing and, seemingly, the number of story writers along with it (despite the diminishing of places to publish the short story), this could be the last time such a national gathering-in of short stories will be read by one person. It is now just about beyond the energy or time of a single editor.

What is gained from a single editor is one mind applying itself to the form and being exposed to the big picture, which provides an opportunity to analyse how the story is being written and about what. I am glad that I did it.

I want to express appreciation for the judgement and standards maintained by our leading literary journals, *Griffith Review, Southerly, Meanjin, Overland, Heat, Island, Westerly, Quadrant* and *Voiceworks*. Interesting work has begun to show up also in the journals published by tertiary departments of writing – *Space* at Deakin University and *Loose Lips* at UTS, to name two.

In arranging the stories I decided to loosely follow the organic order – from stories of youth through to stories of ageing. I think the book reads well if read through this way.

---

### *Some Points of Administrative Clarification*

1  Because of the magnitude of the task, I must apologise for not replying to each entry personally. Only writers who enclosed a SAE received a note from me.

2  Because of the time frame in which I had to read for *Best Australian Stories*, I could not possibly read entire books of stories. I selected one story randomly to read from the books sent to me, and took a similar approach to multiple submissions (the 600 writers submitted about 1000 stories; writers sometimes sent as many as nine stories to read).

3  I am sorry, but time constraints and numbers of stories also made it impossible for me to analyse, comment on or criticise in any detail the stories submitted or to enter into correspondence about them.
It is time for me to get back to my own work.

4 By 'Australian', I took as my guide stories by residents of Australia (for example J.M. Coetzee) or stories written about Australia.

5 I carried over for my selection the stories submitted for the Glen Eira Council competition this year – about 300 pieces – which I judged along with Ian Britain, editor of *Meanjin*.

6 For stories written by my friends or professional acquaintances I used a second reader to help me maintain some detachment – as it turns out, only two of the contributors are known to me.

7 Towards the end of my reading, fearing fatigue or burn-out, I invited two readers (not from publishing and not writing professionals) to sample a random group of the submitted stories. One was a mature-age student in her late thirties and the other was a chef in his early thirties. They read forty stories by twenty-five writers. They broke them into the stories they liked and those they would reject. They rejected twenty stories. In my reading, I had rejected these stories also. Of the eleven writers they thought worth considering, I took four to be considered for the book.

8 A hundred or so submissions were received after the closing date of 1 September and, regrettably, they cannot be read or dealt with. Sorry.

---

### Acknowledgements

I wish to acknowledge the special assistance given to the making of this book by Don Anderson, Tim Herbert, Xavier Hennekinne, Joanna Logue, Andy Logue, Professor Laurie Hergenhan and Sadie-Jane Berenson. I would also like to acknowledge the professional support and advice given by Sophy Williams as publishing manager and Eugenie Baulch of Black Inc. I would like to acknowledge the work done in establishing the series by its inaugural editor, Peter Craven. Finally, I wish to pay tribute to the inspiration of the publisher, Morry Schwartz, without whom the series and its companion titles would not have come into existence and survived.

# After School

## *Nathan Besser*

Gordon's bare feet become black from the loose gravel. The tide breaks softly against the wharf. He smokes tobacco and it stings his tongue like the sherbet he can't believe he still likes. His school shirt is untucked and the wool pants itch at his waist, but he is so used to it he barely notices. The streetlights are dirty yellow in the half moon. He thinks about how much he likes damn girls. Would they ever drift into him as regular as the tides? They stung him like mosquitoes on humid nights, and stuck in his mind like thighs stick to car seats after days at the beach.

When it got painful thinking about all the soft lips that hadn't brushed his neck, he listened more intently to sails chiming against the masts in the harbour. Bugger girls anyway, he thinks. Here I am, listening to the rippling tides. That's better than girls. Kind of.

The last colours from the sun begin to fade. As the day comes to an end, a calm comes to him. A boat wake rocks the jetty posts.

Footsteps come from the path behind. Someone is dragging their feet lazily. Gordon doesn't want anyone to disturb him just as he's finding his equanimity. This is my spot, thinks Gordon. He doesn't turn around, but whoever it is pushes the old tyre that's been tied to the tree. The rope squeaks against the branch like a closing door. Gordon looks. It's a young girl.

\*      \*      \*

The sky is screaming as he hears her stroll around aimlessly. Innumerable questions throw themselves around Gordon's head. Is she looking at me? Do I look OK? Why can't I just enjoy the fucking sky without girls? The sky. The clouds cover the whole sky like vines wrapping a pillar and it is dead still.

She is wearing a blue school skirt and a white T-shirt. Her hair is in a ponytail and frayed strands bundle away from the side of her head. She is tired from her day at school, thinks Gordon, she comes here to be at peace, to think about God and Jazz. How can I impress her? God is a bit hard to make sense of, but I can tell her about that old Duke Ellington video I found at the library. The band wears white suits and Duke clicks his fingers between solos. That's impressive, he thinks.

I just smiled at her. Shit. Did she smile back? Or was that just the moonlight? Either way she is God and I am Jazz. Or something like that anyway. This is happening, really happening. I never had a girl. But I have a brain and passion and all the things that matter. Shit. She just smiled back at me.

\*      \*      \*

'Hey.'

'Hey.' Gordon can barely talk. 'It's nice here ay?'

'Yeah, I like coming here sometimes when I get sick of homework.' As she speaks she scratches her knee. She sits on the wall and her legs swing to and fro. One of her shoelaces is undone and the bit at the end hits the wall softly.

'Me too. I just thought to come and say hi. Fellow school students, you know. I'm Gordon.'

'Nice to meet ya. I'm Kathryn.' Her hair is blonde, she is snub-nosed and grubby. She is beautiful.

'Nice to meet you.'

'So, what school d'ya go to?' She speaks ocker.

'This weird one ages away. It's called Moriah. You probably haven't heard of it. You?'

'Rozelle Public. So is yours like a private one or what?'

'Ummm, yeah. It's Jewish.'

'Aww. So are you a Jew?'

'Yeah.'

'I don't know anythin about Jews. Do you go to like a church on Sundays?'

'Not really. My family isn't religious. But my grandparents survived the Holocaust and it's important to my parents that I grow up a bit Jewish.'

'Cool.'

There is roaring silence as she plays with her fingernails. Her skin is soft and her legs are slim. Gordon dips his feet in the water to impress her. She asks if it's nice and he assures her it is. She takes off her shoes and dips her feet in. Both their feet are bare. Nothing could be more intimate.

'So. You gotta girlfriend?'

'Nah. Just broke up a few weeks ago.' It's a lie, but he can't tell her he hasn't even kissed a girl. 'You?'

'Kinda. But nothin really. I don't like, heaps like him.' She makes swirls in the water with her big toe. The flickering puddle sounds are deafening.

Two fishermen come in their big black gumboots and stand on the rocks. Gordon hears the occasional laugh, but otherwise they mind their business. They pull out bait from an old paint bucket. He hears the line whistle through the reel as they cast out and then silence and then … plop.

'Ya like to fish?'

'I never really did it properly. Just with a hand reel. You?'

'Yeah, sometimes. Dad loves it. But it's slow and bawrin. I prefer boys. Haha.' Gordon doesn't know whether to be disgusted or turned on. But he laughs with her and nothing could spoil this.

'So what music do you like?'

'Umm, all different stuff I guess. Like Today FM and Top 40, but sometimes classical. Mum loves classical and it helps me sleep. I love that Beethoven fella. He's real relaxing. You?'

'Everything too. But I really love Jazz. You know, like Duke Ellington?'

'Haven't hearda him.'

Gordon tells her all about him and she thinks it sounds kinda cool and weird. He likes telling her that black men make the best music and have the best rhythm. He wants to hold her.

\*     \*     \*

*For the fishermen it is a deathly calm afternoon in perfect heat.*

*Dead mosquitoes are stuck to the inside of the street lamps, and dust and grime collect on the underneath of the glass. Work is finished for the week and there is no better way to wind down. It's also nice to know about the tides and the tackle and what sort of fish you might catch round this part of the harbour.*

*Two school children sit on the breakwater and dangle their legs in the water. Crumpled white socks are falling out of a pair of black school shoes next to them. The boy nervously says something to the girl as he looks down at the water and she doesn't look up, but he puts his arm around her and she rests her head on his shoulder.*

\*     \*     \*

Gordon's heart is beating so hard against his ribcage that his body shakes with every pulse. The terror is the joy of having her. She seems so unflustered by the situation. A real natural, he thinks.

'I gotta get home for tea.' She doesn't move her head from his shoulder as she speaks.

'Yeah. Me too. My Mum has probably sent out a search party for me.'

'I hate when my parents get worried.'

'So you wanna meet here again tomorrow?' He can barely breathe as he asks the question.

'Yeah, howz about five in the arvo?'

'Cool. I'll lend you the Duke Ellington movie. It's so cool. Johnny Hodges is on it as well.'

'Well it's been real nice. I won't tell my boyfriend about ya. He is a loser anyway, I'm gonna dump him.' She pulls her head off his shoulder, and the pain from being so still slowly fades. She doesn't look at him, but her lips are all of a sudden against his. It is warm and soft and overwhelming. Once the shock subsides he manages to stroke her hair.

They say goodbye and she saunters off with her shoes in her hand.

\*       \*       \*

The pavement feels nice on Gordon's feet and the splintering telegraph poles stretch all the way to heaven. The cicadas are loud and the birds are talking their heads off before darkness sets in. Mum bothers him about homework and dinner and being clean, but he can't get away from the tingling in his mouth. The heat from her tongue is still making its way around the corners of his mouth.

There is nothing until tomorrow afternoon but the drum in his chest and the memory of her mouth. He gazes at the ceiling for five hours.

\*       \*       \*

The next day he waits for two hours but she doesn't come.

Gordon waits every day for three weeks but she never comes.

He thinks that it is because of her boyfriend but he can't fight the feeling that there is something wrong with him.

The harbour stays calm for the month that he goes to the wharf. The fishermen come on Fridays. At sundown the birds gather around the tree that has the old tyre tied to it. They fly from branch to branch with such agility, he thinks. They become like insects. Gordon sometimes swings on the old tyre. There is a bubbler just at the entrance to the jetty path. He drinks from it as an excuse for being there so often.

He begins to swim even though it's dirty and no one ever swims there. The barnacles and molluscs make his feet even rougher than they already are. The crabs scuttle around like his mother's fingernails on the glass table. Sometimes he sings Ellington tunes and waves to the ferry drivers.

\*       \*       \*

*It's the end of the week and they go fishing together as always. They take the usual path to the jetty beneath the powerlines that hang silently in the heat.*

*The fish have been biting solidly for a month and the conditions are relentlessly still. The kid is still sitting on the wharf. One day his Mum comes and leads him away. He seems to be crying.*

*The fishermen wedge their rods in between the cracks of the break-water. They hover against the sky like antennas. An occasional bite comes and they reel in. A boat drives past, breaking the lingering buzz of cicadas. It sends ripples that rock the old jetty posts.*

# Unfinished Business

## *Susan Coleridge*

Misty drizzle falls beyond the terminal lights. Typical, she thinks, for it to be raining in Melbourne when Sydney was ablaze with sunshine. The taxi draws in beside her. She slides into the back seat, her overnight bag getting tangled in her legs, and gives her address. The car glides away from the brilliance of the airport onto the gleaming freeway.

Absently she gazes into the night at the predictable urban landscape. Illuminated billboards and factories subside with the onset of suburbia. The imposing pillars of the city shine in the distance. In Sydney it is much the same – this trip from the airport – only shorter.

Charlie had thought of everything and even though part of her had been expecting it, his proposal still came as a surprise. For one brief moment Anna glimpses her life as it could be – the light-filled house, the pool, the friends and of course the children.

Cars slip by, lights flick at her face. The taxi feels sealed, secure, removed from the life surrounding it – a continuation of the vacuum she has been in all weekend. Through her mind she runs the telephone call she will make when she gets home. She rehearses the things she will say, the things he will say.

Something brings her back to the cabin of the taxi. The

driver has been looking at her. She can still feel his gaze. She glances quickly in his direction but his eyes are back on the road. In the slit of the rear-vision mirror they are narrowed in concentration. Anna sits a little lower and fishes a diary from her handbag. She'll be ready if he tries it again. She doesn't like being watched.

She stares at the diary. It makes her feel less exposed, less vulnerable to unplanned conversations.

The car hums as it journeys through the night. After a while she relaxes a little, lets her eyes slide back to the window and her mind slip back to her thoughts.

'Good weekend?'

It's him again – the driver. It seems his scrutiny was a precursor to conversation. She feels something close to dismay.

'Yes, thanks.' Polite but unencouraging. She looks down at her diary and turns a page as if searching for something.

'You don't remember me, do you?'

Startled, her head jerks up.

'What?'

'Sorry, didn't mean to surprise you like that.'

He doesn't sound sorry.

Somehow the voice is familiar. She looks again in the rear-vision mirror. So are the eyes.

'Rob,' he says as if in answer. 'Rob Wiseman – Strathfield High.'

She stares back into the mirror, the penny still dropping.

'About ten years ago,' he adds. 'You taught me once. Maybe you don't remember.'

Her first year teaching had been in the north-west. The town was dull as only small country towns can be. The land-scape surrounding it was flat, windswept, virtually treeless. Each day, even in winter, had seemed to be endlessly bright and warm – like the people. They had been kind, sensing her alienation, but it had been her first experience of loneliness, of boredom – relentless and numbing. For years after she had been depressed by blue skies.

'I remember,' she replies carefully. 'It's a while ago though.'

'Yeah.'

Anna drops her eyes and shifts slightly in the back seat, angling away from him. He has surprised her. More than she cares to admit. She coughs and runs her fingers through her hair.

'You still teaching?' he asks.

She is still absorbing the fact of who he is, so she doesn't answer immediately. He catches her eye in the mirror, raises an eyebrow. She remembers his question.

'Yes. Not kids though.'

'Not kids,' he repeats.

She smiles quickly, acknowledging the irony. Even ten years ago he hadn't been a kid.

'Oh, I mean, I teach adults now. No one under eighteen – well, rarely.'

Annoyed, she hears the old hesitancy in her voice. Her voice would do that back then. Somewhere inside her a pulse has started.

'Anyway, what about you? Did you do year twelve?' She tries to sound interested but detached.

'Yeah. I was an OK student. You might remember that.'

She hears the mockery in his voice. It is very faint but it is there. His academic ability is not what she remembers.

She hadn't found teaching easy – especially at the beginning. The students weren't novices like her. She'd exuded inexperience and uncertainty. It had started badly when one of the girls – a sharp-eyed redhead called Andrea – had asked her why she wasn't wearing a uniform. Almost apologetically she'd explained that she was the teacher. Hotness had crept over her and Andrea's smirk had rippled around the room.

'So, after year twelve?' She meets his eyes briefly.

'Nothing much really.'

'You didn't go on to anything else?'

'No – not then. Could've though. I was accepted into Law at Monash.'

'Really?' Anna is impressed. 'Why didn't you go?'

'The old man died,' he says. 'Just dropped dead one afternoon in the yards. Heart attack.'

'I'm sorry.'

'Yeah. Only fifty-two and fit – so we all thought. I guess he
can't have been.'

'So you ran the farm?'

'Yeah, I didn't really have a choice. I couldn't leave Mum.'

'No, I guess not.'

She turns back to the window. The car is warm and feels
too intimate. The damp cityscape beyond the window seems
a long way from the arid, sun-soaked paddocks of Strathfield.
It seems a long way from Sydney too.

The traffic is busier. She hears Rob mutter an expletive as
a truck overtakes them. The rush of air it produces buffets the
car and the windscreen is sprayed with fine, greasy water.

They reach the Bolte Bridge. Its spot-lit concrete columns
rear in the urban night and they drive across it in silence.
Almost silence. The two-way radio is vibrating with arrange-
ments.

Out of the corner of her eye she can see the shape of his
head. She remembers when, in order to avoid his gaze, she
would stand at the back of the classroom. His ears are folded
neatly against his skull and his neck is elegant. She tries
to concentrate on Charlie, on Sydney, on their combined
future, but it is as though Rob's head, his neck blocks her. He
fills the car the way he had filled that classroom. She turns
towards him.

'And then?'

'What?' It is his turn to be surprised.

'So you ran the farm. Then what?'

'Yeah ... right ... the farm.' He pauses. It is as if he has been
away somewhere. 'It was hard. I didn't realise how hard until
things started going wrong – I won't bore you with the
details.' He stops, sighs. 'So we sold up and moved into town.
Well, Mum did. I came down here. Mucked around for a few
years – bar work, taxi driving and then I decided to get serious, so I started Law.'

Anna hears his words but she is more conscious of his hands – one is on the steering wheel, the other rests on the automatic transmission lever. His hands look strong – farmer's hands, she thinks.

A beat of time passes before she continues.

'Not easy,' she says.

'No, it wasn't.' He sighs again. 'Not an original story, though. And I guess Law will get me a lot further than farming.'

'I guess,' she agrees.

They have reached the river. It glimmers darkly like shot silk. As they drive along Alexandra Avenue she gazes vaguely at the glitter of the city. At the Swan Street Bridge the lights turn red. The left-hand indicator winks at her in the darkness.

'You said Richmond, didn't you?'

'Yes. It's not far.'

He nods, then looks at her in the mirror. Right at her.

'And what about you?'

The lights change and the car moves. His eyes go back to the road.

'Me?' Her mouth is dry.

'Yeah. Where'd you go after Strathfield?'

And then, abruptly, she is back there – in the hot school hall where they had that final assembly. The principal had announced the names of those who would be leaving. When her name was spoken she remembers glancing over at him and seeing the surprise, maybe even shock in his eyes. He'd looked back at her and then he'd looked away. She hadn't seen him again.

Until now.

'Oh, I just came back to Melbourne,' she says eventually.

'Did you keep teaching?'

'Yes … I'd applied for a transfer.'

'To another school?'

'Yes.'

'So … you wanted to go?'

'Yes.'

'Right.' He pauses and seems to consider what she has said. 'I guess there wasn't much to keep you in Strathfield.'

'Not really.'

There is silence again, but this time there is uneasiness in it. Anna feels the need to break it. Ridiculously she feels that somehow she has hurt his feelings.

'I was transferred to a school in the western suburbs,' she offers.

'Good?' His voice gives away nothing.

'It was a tough school. I didn't last there long. I couldn't cope really.'

'You weren't really coping in Strathfield,' he says quietly.

She stops. She hadn't expected him to say that. She feels cut off, like a boat drifting into uncharted waters. She feels his eyes on her again.

'Was it that obvious?' she murmurs.

'To me it was.'

His last words hang in the air needing to be defused, stripped of meaning.

In something near desperation she turns to speak. Instead she meets his eyes again, leaving unsaid the words that could save her. The atmosphere stretches thin and tight between them as the car nears its destination. They drive down Bridge Road and then into the narrow side street where she lives.

'Number twenty-three?' he says. His voice is husky.

'Yes,' she replies unsteadily.

The car stops in front of her narrow Victorian terrace.

'Nice place,' he comments.

'Thanks,' she says. 'What do I owe you?'

'Nothing. It's on me.'

'You can't do that.'

'Watch me.'

'Please.' Anna pushes the money towards him.

'The meter's not on.' He stares straight ahead. Anna bites her lip, the hand proffering the note stranded in midair.

'Why?' she asks.

'Because I want to,' he replies tightly.

'There's no need.'

'I know.'

She sits for a moment considering her next move. There are things that can be said but she won't say them. Neither will he.

'Well … thank you.'

She collects her bags and opens the door. The coolness of the night breezes into the car.

'Well, goodbye, and … good luck with everything.'

He nods and then quickly twists around. This time when his eyes meet hers she doesn't look away. Seconds pass, then he passes something to her.

'Call me if you need another ride.' He smiles. 'Special rates.'

'Like tonight,' she quips weakly.

'Yeah, something like that.'

She takes the card. As their fingertips brush, a prickle of heat passes up her arm.

'I'd better go,' she breathes.

'Yeah.' He turns back to the dashboard and says roughly, 'See you 'round.'

Anna feels stupid, as if she's been dismissed. She manages to get out of the cab a little more gracefully than she had got in. For a moment she stands, swaying slightly in the drizzle. Then the passenger window slides down. He dips his head so she can see him. The streetlight shines on his face. This time she avoids his eyes.

'I'll wait till you're inside,' he says. His voice, although neutral, is tinged with both apology and regret.

'Oh, OK … thanks.'

The garden gate creaks as she pushes it open. Needs oil, she thinks absently. She finds her key, eases the door open and turns on the passage light. He is still waiting in the street. From her lit doorway she turns and waves briefly. The taxi begins to cruise slowly up the street. She watches it until it turns into Bridge Road and is gone. She sighs and closes the door behind her. For minutes she stands there leaning against the door with her eyes closed. After a while she picks up her bags and moves to the staircase.

In the bedroom the orange light of the answer phone blinks. She looks beyond it to the city skyline lit like a Christmas tree. The view is spectacular. She wonders where he is now in that explosion of light. She sighs again and presses the button. Charlie's voice spills into the room.

'Hello darling.' She winces slightly. 'Missing you dreadfully already. Hope you had a good trip home. Speak tomorrow. I love you.'

Anna doesn't ring back.

Eventually she goes to bed.

She is still awake when the phone rings.

'It's Rob,' he says.

The shock of his voice jolts her. Her heart begins pounding. She tries to steady herself before she speaks. Her throat is dry.

'Hello.' Her voice is cracked and oddly high-pitched.

'You left a … it looks like a diary – on the back seat.'

'Oh – right.' She can hardly speak.

'Your phone number is in it – just inside the cover.'

'Yes … it's my work diary.'

'I thought it might be important.'

'It is …'

'I hope it's all right.'

'What?'

'I meant, to ring now. I hope it was OK.' There is uncertainty in his voice.

'Yes – of course,' she croaks.

There is a long silence.

'It's late,' she says finally.

'Were you asleep?'

'No.'

Another silence. She can hear the radio voices in his car.

'I – I'll leave it in your letterbox at the end of my shift.' He sounds tentative, as if she's caught him off guard.

Anna breathes deeply, aware that she is standing on the brink of a chasm. She need go no further. All she has to say is OK and she will have moved back from the precipice. Back to safe territory where the ground is predictable, where the going is steady, secure – where Charlie is and the rest of her life lies. Clutching the phone, she props herself up against the pillows. She feels the glow of the city lighting her face and sparking her eyes.

'No,' she says. 'Don't do that.'

He says nothing. Yet another silence, but this one more dangerous.

'Come now,' she says. 'I think you should come now.'

# Letter to the Drowned

## *Nathan Besser*

You have become part of it. Part of the water. Our last time
together, we were surrounded by water. It became everything,
became you. The thick, weightless calm it gave your body. I
remember your arms floating beside you, and a snake of
bubbles leaving your mouth, approaching the surface. I can't
drive the image from my mind.

I'd watch you smoke on the back step. Your eyelids wincing
as you pulled smoke into your mouth. The crackle of burning tobacco and the simultaneous glow, illuminating your
face. You only smoked once a day. It was always on the back
step, alone. Usually around 11 p.m. Sometimes on weekends,
it would be when the sun was rising. You seemed happiest in
summer, when the cicadas buzzed and the air was tepid. Did
you know I watched you every time?

I remember our first meeting like it was yesterday. We spoke
for half an hour about how much we hated parties. We were
at a party. You were wearing a white skirt and a blouse. Your
hair fell around your shoulders. We escaped and swam
together in Gordon's Bay. The water was cold and we shivered
and laughed. I remember thinking that such serendipity was
only reserved for drunkenness. Was I right? Maybe the past

fifteen years were drunken. Now that it is gone, that you are gone, that I am gone, I consider it possible.

\*　　\*　　\*

On the days that I noticed it, I never mentioned it. But I wanted to. The sea was rising, but you wouldn't have believed me. Or even worse, you would have dismissed it as unimportant. I felt the rising tide most intensely when you went to the toilet in the middle of the night. I always woke up. Your flat feet on the carpet. The twisted, creased sheets which marked your empty space on our bed. I always wondered what you did in the bathroom. Sometimes you were gone for half an hour or even more. It was at those times I first felt the tide. The sound of the waves growing louder beyond our window. The spreading white of a broken wave reaching closer and closer towards us like tentacles.

And when you returned to bed, as you always did, it felt like part of you was left behind. If you noticed I was awake, you put your hand on my forehead. You had renewed energy to touch me. But it didn't last long. You kissed me as a mother kisses her child and then fell back asleep. I asked you if the waves seemed louder, but you said no, they didn't seem louder.

I woke up each morning with a strange feeling. It felt like I had crushed something delicate in my sleep. I woke up scared to move. Scared to make further damage. And each night I fell asleep, wary. I was lying on a bed of glass. What could I do? Do you know how awful it was to feel powerless?

I don't know why these things come to mind. They are scattered, living things. They are not memories, because they still breathe as living things do. And now you will read them, and the pages will become part of the water. The pulp will emulsify into nothing. I sometimes wonder if it's the same water that we swam in, that first time we met. Maybe I began drowning then and failed to see it?

\*   \*   \*

At first when I took my daily stroll along the beach, I thought the tides were simply in a high cycle. But then, I found myself retreating further and further towards the base of the escarpment. I didn't think much of it – it was normal for these things to happen. We discussed it one morning when we swam together. Once again you said nothing had changed. I presumed you were right. Often, I thought you were right.

You used to wear that straw hat when you worked outside. It lasted so long, that hat. The meshed, white straw made an arced shadow on your face. There were sparkles of light mingled amongst the shadow. You were good to those children. You built a child-care centre out of the back of our house. I thought that was a good idea.

When I occasionally left my work to help you with the children, I was always amazed at your kindness. It was effortless. The way you stroked their heads and took them by the hand and lifted them onto your hip. I wished I could have brought you children of your own. I can't imagine how much you wanted your own child. You said it didn't matter. I didn't believe you.

It was not long after that when the ocean climbed even higher. I had to jump off the rocks to swim. The beach had disappeared. I didn't really mind. The feeling of moss and barnacles under my feet pleased me. They became brown and calloused. I opened my eyes under the water when it was clear, and swam with the fish. I guess I made the most of it. You didn't want to swim very much anymore.

\*   \*   \*

When your mother died, I didn't understand how deeply it affected you. I just supposed your grief lasted a long time. But I think, maybe, you were grieving for more than your mother.

Her funeral was small. There was only a handful of people. You and I, and your brother's family. You stayed up all night talking with him. You sat on the couch with your legs curled up under you. It was nice to see you with your family. There were faint bags under your eyes, and redness in your cheeks. I remember seeing strands of your curly, dark hair sticking to your face from tears. Your lips were swollen from crying. I thought you looked beautiful. You came to me for comfort. I held you and you trembled in my arms. Why did I enjoy that so much?

Soon after, the water was only a few metres from our home. It had risen up the escarpment, where our house was perched. The one thing we equally loved. The sound of the children playing in the back. The weatherboards that we repainted every five years. The old tyre swing which your brother's children loved more than the both of us put together. The weathervane that became rusty from the sea air. Our red front door. It really was a beautiful home.

I couldn't swim anymore and you closed the day-care centre. The water was lapping at our backdoor. Thick, rising swirls of sea foam against our window. I didn't want to mention it. I figured you were still grieving. We lay in our home, silently. You smoked in the lounge room. The wisps of smoke climbing over the bookcase.

Water started trickling through the roof, and between the cracks of the walls. It dripped from the ceiling in solitary beads. The sound reminded me of your feet on the carpet. I tried holding you, but you just lit another cigarette. You never told me to leave you alone. I felt like a fawning pet nagging at your leg. I said we needed to leave to survive. You didn't agree, and you didn't disagree. All our time, I had wanted your loyalty. And now, I could only have it in death.

I tried holding the water in pots and pans. It was a last

desperate attempt to contain it. But it didn't work. They overflowed quickly. The popping sound of water on water was deafening. I could see thick currents churning against our windows. Seaweed washed past, and rocks rolled underneath our foundations with the sound of an abacus.

I threatened to leave. I wanted us to leave together. You said you wouldn't. We were drowning, I said. You said it didn't matter. I wanted to take you, but you wouldn't come. You were indifferent. I broke through the bedroom window as the water climbed towards our ceiling. Your hair was swimming around you slowly. It looked like the seaweed at our window. Light filtered through the water. Your pale skin was blue, almost transparent.

You were looking at me as I swam towards the surface, my lungs burning. You wouldn't move. Our eyes met. You looked away and I broke through the surface, gasping.

# jump

## *Erin Gough*

Like a fever breaking. Like being shaken awake. It's the moment of whiplash in a car crash. It's inertia finally slapping you in the face.

There's the black sky, the black surface below and you with your toes on the railing between. When jumping at night you can feel the water even before you meet it blind. The fall from the bridge to the canal is never far, but it's far enough for you to know the buzz of hollow air and the cold of what's to come and to ask the questions that can send you more numb than the water ever will: what if it's not deep enough? what if I fall too fast? And almost before you've asked these things you're heavy in the depths of it and already choking and spitting and lashing your way to the surface.

But you get there, eventually, and you say Christ, and fucking hell, and haul yourself out with mud on your clothes.

And after that, you do it all again.

### hot baby wild

The night I meet Cushla is the night I get fired from the Q

Store, and it's hot, so hot I'm having trouble moving down the street. The salt and chips air is thicker than pub smoke, the footpath is cracking under my toes, but despite it all, there I am, walking shoeless in the dark, with the exhilaration known only to those who have been recently made redundant.

Half an hour ago under fluorescent lighting, I discovered that you can't swear at a customer and not lose your job; that this is especially the case when the customer in question is married to your boss; and that if that's the way it's going to be, then there's space enough in the security camera's blind spot at the end of aisle three to stash half a dozen videos into your backpack and make off with them without being caught.

And so it is that I come upon Cushla in the writhing summer heat on the slow way home an hour before my usual finish-up time: with stolen goods in my bag, and an urge to do something wild.

She is walking in front of me, water dripping from the ends of her hair and down her back. She has a long-sleeved shirt with jeans that meet heavy boots at her ankles. From the way she is stopping at corners, I can tell she is lost.

What I cannot tell is that she will become my distraction. That for almost two months, in place of boredom, she will be the thing I live and eat and breathe. Right now all I am certain of is that I have never in my life come across anybody wearing more clothes on such a crazy-hot night, than this damp and dizzy girl, this trick of light.

**the neighbourhood**

But first of all, the neighbourhood.

The neighbourhood you need to know about, because it is part of the endless heat, the long days, the water-logged nights that follow. The neighbourhood is what makes things dull enough to fall out of.

The neighbourhood must come first because it was here first, only by a short while, but by enough to make all that comes afterwards contingent upon it. For two months it is our nature and our nurture, Cushla's and mine. What we are, and will become, has everything to do with it.

First of all with its broad, open streets and three-storeyed houses, most of them built by car retailers, or jam manufac-turers, or magazine magnates simply to shift merchandise: This stunning, classically modern Roman-Scandinavian villa with fully landscaped gardens located less than half an hour from the world's most spectacular beaches could be yours. Just buy ten bottles of your favourite tonic water to enter the draw and begin your new life in paradise on the Gold Coast.

In between the prize-homes are the manufactured greens that the brochures call parklands or common gardens. There are roundabouts topped with bonsais. There are ornamental fountains. Then snaking right through the middle of every-thing in this neighbourhood that breeds us – through the greens, between the houses, through the broad, open streets – are the waterways. These come to shape us above everything else.

The canals we make our own, because nobody has claimed them yet. They are the space between other places, there to provide that shimmery real estate ideal known as the 'water-view'. Mere accessories to this greater cause, not things in themselves. Not to anyone, that is, but Cushla and me.

A street away from one of these waterways, near the corner of Havana Road and Sanctuary Drive, Cushla finally turns around on that sweltering night, and asks me where she is. She hasn't a clue, she's lost herself entirely, the streets go around in circles, it seems to her. She smiles at me, and wipes the damp hair out of her face with the back of a sleeve.

Where do you need to go? I ask.

Her eyes turn away for a moment. Cargo Street, she says finally.

I can help her with Cargo Street. I know it because my brother works as a nurse in the hospital there. But just before we reach it, as we are crossing the bridge on Killinger Road, she stops. I turn around to see her leaning on the railing looking straight at me.

Have you ever jumped off one of these bridges? she asks.

I laugh. It's a long way down.

I watch her lift herself up and climb over the railing, onto the narrow stretch of concrete on the other side. She turns to face me. With her hands holding tight she swings backwards until the length of her body is stretched out over the water. I watch as her fingers slip gradually from between the vertical bars.

Standing on the bridge, wanting to know what will happen next, I do nothing, at first. I wait for her to disappear. At any moment I expect she will be gone, that the water will collect her, that she will drop away as if she were never there at all. But the more I wait for her, the more, it seems, she waits for me.

Come on, she says at last.

The railing is almost too high to get over. I push myself up with my hands, and then haul my legs across, until I am finally on the ledge beside her.

She grins then, and almost at once I am watching her twist and leap into the heavy air, her arms outstretched, the wide sky against her back.

**days**

I wake to the sound of engines. Outside the sun is beating the landscape white. I shift my head in half-sleep, feel the dampness of the pillow; remember.

There are trucks on the street; they are building another mansion. I go out into the garden to watch the men lift ceramic basins, cane lounges, peach-coloured carpet in double-jointed rolls. When they leave, I climb through a window and into the living room. I run my palms along the lacquered pine table-for-four. I take off my shoes and stretch out on the settee, pressing my toes into spotless cushions. The house feels gutted, the air stale; once outside again I am dizzy and unsteady on my feet.

My summer, now lacking the certainty provided by regular work hours, becomes imbued with this rhythm – a series of suffocations and resurfacings: empty houses followed by wide open streets; wakefulness followed by afternoon sleep; hot days followed by night, and everything that night brings with it: the cooling dark, the water, Cushla.

Having lost the Q Store job I begin spending time following my brother in and out of hospital wards carrying thermometers and bedpans. This is where I find her again. In the steel-framed bed she looks limp, and paler than I remember, her expression disengaged. I stand beside my brother as he talks to her and she glances about without listening. I search for recognition on her face; I find none. But when my brother turns away momentarily to read her chart, she looks straight at me, propping her head against the pillow, and grins.

Any new aches or pains to report? my brother asks her, glancing up from his clipboard.

Her face becomes sullen. Right here, she tells him, pointing to her nose. Right on the bridge.

As she says 'bridge' her eyes flit back to meet mine. She bites at her bottom lip. My brother writes it down with the stub of a hospital pencil. I stand beside him, wanting to laugh out loud.

**nights**

We agree to meet on Palm Street, where the bridge is concrete and steel and two lanes wide; where the cars roll past anonymous, their headlights leaving you blind at intervals.

On the first night I wait there over an hour. My house key is heavy in my shorts pocket; it is on a ring I've safety-pinned to the inside. Under the togs beneath my clothes, my skin is damp. By ten o'clock, she hasn't come. I turn to peer at the dark water below, and think about going home.

Five minutes later she appears from nowhere, grinning and panting. Five minutes after that she has already leapt into the water, and is shouting at me to get a move on. Does the hospital know where you are? I hear myself ask, but the cars are roaring by, and she is splashing and ducking, and doesn't answer.

Come on, is all she yells.

I laugh into the noise of my racing blood, into a mouthful of water that finds me in the quiet world beneath the surface, until I pull myself up through the fog to meet her shrieks of delight. She swims over to me and pushes me down further, her hands firm on my shoulders, my face against her neck.

She holds me like this until I need to draw breath. I struggle against her grip. She holds me a moment longer. Just in time she releases me, and I gasp for air. Then she is at the edge, heaving herself and her streaming clothes onto the embankment, ready to go again.

The bridge at the end of Haven Street, or the one in the middle of Tropical Road; night after night we fall off the edge of every place we can. Sometimes the levels seem too low, but Cushla doesn't appear to care. She always jumps first, and I know that if she didn't I would lack the courage, and probably the inclination. Part of me wants the thrill of the fall, but mostly I need to follow Cushla; to take the water into my mouth to belong to it, to belong to her.

Afterwards we sit along the edge of the road rolling pieces of gravel under the palms of our hands. When she stretches for more pieces, out of her long, damp sleeves, I notice scars on her arms, her wrists; streaks of silver. I wonder how they got there and what the skin feels like at those places, but I never ask. We talk instead about the best bridges to jump: the ones where there is the least traffic, or where the water is clearest. And on the way home we follow the canals past the rows of mansions, standing so huge and silent that we submit to their speechlessness. At these times we carry our thoughts like secrets along the steady dark ribbon, to the beat of the crickets and the sound of squelching shoes.

**houses**

It is a heat-soaked night in January and we have jumped three bridges in a row, but still it doesn't seem enough. I am awake and energetic, and decide to keep Cushla from disappearing.

I've got something to show you, I say to her.

I lead her through the flat empty streets. We are still dripping wet as we climb through the window of the vacant mansion, into the stale air and a room full of unused furniture.

How do you know about this place? she asks as we feel our way through the darkness.

I've walked past it, that's all.

Cushla slides her bum onto the lacquered table and swings her legs over the edge. She looks around. This house is huge, she says, grabbing my hands. We should have a party here.

Yeah right, I say. Like no one'd notice.

Are you serious? Cushla grins. Nobody cares. We can do anything we want.

What do you want to do, then? I ask.

Oh anything, she says. It doesn't matter to me.

That's when I touch her face with my hand, letting my fingers rest on her cheek, the silence of the room beating around me. She laughs, and asks me what I am doing. Then she pushes herself off the table, and I stumble backwards to let her pass as she moves towards the door. It opens with a siren sound; the house alarm. Cushla shrieks against the noise. Come on then, she cries.

I stand there drenched, as she races down the street.

**into the water**

The last night I spend with Cushla is a Thursday at the end of summer. Running out of bridges, we head to a place we have never been; to a street that leads to the city. The road is high over the water. From the bridge we can see its surface deep down in the bunker of the canal.

We take off our shoes. Cushla bends into the shadows and slips through the narrow bars. Hurry up, she calls to me, or I'll lose my nerve.

Looking at the waterway, crusted at the edges and muddied with silt, I can tell it's not deep enough. What are you waiting for? she asks me from the ledge.

I stare at her, incredulous. It's too dangerous.

She considers me for a moment, and then lets her gaze fall back upon the water. I'm doing it anyway, I don't care, she says at last, and that's when I realise she doesn't.

She turns around to face it, her hands freed, balancing on her heels. I want to shout out, but she is already in the air.

The water shimmers, licking itself black and sounding like thunder that strikes the moment she arrives, the moment it welcomes her. I stand back from the edge with my breath caught in my chest, barely wanting to see.

The water is a still mirror. There is only the sound of cars on the road. Cushla is nowhere at all. I hear a splash, and she is hauling herself up to the surface beneath me; she is under the bridge in the shade of the already-dark.

The surface of the canal rolls and shudders. I hear her laughter resonating between the concrete walls. She calls out to me. I don't answer her. High on the bridge, with the cars roaring past on their way to the city, I am bending down for my shoes, picking them up by their laces, carrying them home.

# the american dream

*i.j. oog*

**prologue**

last night i dreamt i had a round smooth ceramic handle on my back and it was interchangeable with other smooth ceramic handles in a range of sizes – you were lying beside me as you had been all night your beautiful mouth your clear eyes closed

*i am so tired lately* he says *i sleep a lot normally when i am not with you i mean*

she returns his crooked smile generously – her perfect teeth showing the benefit of everything the american dental profession has to offer and i wonder briefly if they'd have fluoridation in america – of course they would: a lifetime of fluoridation

he says: *the point is that you are special but i am mindful of the possibility that in the long term i would tire of that which amuses me in you now: the child in you – and you would get bored with me: always tired – too often cynical – i am not a hero – i've said that before and what good did it do then eh?*

i am struggling to find a voice with which to speak to her – we are talking about poetry – when she asks who is your favourite poet i am tempted to say walt disney but i say: *i don't read poetry it is too complicated and like nietzsche i tire of poets old and new – but i still write it and it is a perfect extension of the self … no not the self but a self … into life and time even when i bury it in prose*

it finally started raining last night – for hours only the most tentative of droplets fell but slowly and steadily it set in and now twenty-four hours later it is thick and solid and keeps on coming down – when i drive home in the dark there is plenty of water running off the road out of town but there is plenty staying on it too – in ridges that catch under the car

**one**

*do you want to come in my mouth* she asks having brought me to the point of orgasm with her lips her tongue her perfect teeth and one hand around the base of my cock the other cupped around my balls – *or in my cunt?*

call me an unrepentant child of the tv generation but i love america – or perhaps it is the idea of america that i love – and these soft round american vowels with a slight southern lilt produce in me the expectation of a special secret sauce and this is what made america great: something is offered and accepted – a choice is offered and a choice is made and it is not a choice between good and bad or even good and better – each option is good and good and good the best and i'll tell you this is the best america has to offer – she is winona ryder no wait she is a cross between her and lauren bacall and she is right here on my thin mattress on the ground in my little room in this dilapidated farmhouse in the middle of nowhere and it is like a fucking theme park

*you tremble when you come* i say – she is lying there quietly – the shape of her mouth makes me hard again – it was only the second time i had seen her come and the first time i was drunk and desperate to come myself but this time i was fucking her slowly with a good hard cock and flicking my tongue fast across her nipple and telling her how beautiful she is and saying *yes i want to fuck you in the arse* when she asks *do you want to fuck me in the arse* and *yes i want to come in your arse* when she asks *do you want to come in my arse?*

i feel like getting her to say the names of all the american cities i can think of while i fuck her – i think about the practicalities of it:

*lasvegassanfransiscodetroitnewyorkbostonchicagoalbuquerquewashingtonneworleansoklahomacitykansas*

i think about asking her to take a year off and drive with me across america and to go to all the towns and cities whose names i have ever heard and to fuck her and send myself a postcard from each and every one

i am like a vampire a living dead man i need feminine energy to make me feel alive and i absorb it unashamedly as if by osmosis even as i sleep it seeps into me – i am needy but as i said to her *needs and expectations are your own responsibility* and so i don't go looking for her when she disappears – i wait for her to find me

it is as if she senses it: she is careful not to spend too much time with me – she arrives late at night and leaves early in the morning – and i am aware of it too – my tired fucked-up body is greedy – it wants to drink and drink and drink from that fountain take it all in quickly

i say: *now! tonight! come and sleep with me tonight* – she says *i might pass i've got a lot of work on* – the body replies with a trickle of disappointment bordering on distress like a junkie who has obtained some temporary energy from the hope that he is going to get a hit soon – i feel faint – i am ready to collapse – everything is a long long way away and i am aching aching

**two**

the whole landscape has changed with all this rain the ground is saturated and the colours more intense the shapes of the trees alter with the weight of the water – when i go for a walk all the rusty fragments of machinery around the sheds look exquisitely beautiful

it is a simple fact of life that woman offers the most benign of possible interactions with the other but she having offered a few drops of love to a parched desert dweller should be spared the full ferocity of his thirst

she keeps asking me what the time is what date is it what week are we in how long before school finishes – i say: *what am i? the speaking clock? if you are so interested in time get yourself a watch get yourself a calendar*

little orange mushrooms have sprouted all around the cow-pats – i squeeze the stem of one: it seems to turn purple like it should

it made me sick to the stomach to stand there (or maybe it was when we were sitting in the car) and to ask her if she wanted to come home with me – it being such a cold night with the fog rolling in – i had just got a heap of firewood and a couple of bottles of that not-too-bad pinot noir

is there a space between poetry and prose – is there a space between beauty and truth … fiction and reality? is it possible to write or speak from a point of view which straddles the real and the imaginary and perhaps even the symbolic … no not the symbolic … forget the goddamn symbolic … there are too many symbols and too many people fingering them …

but yes perhaps you were right – perhaps it is better that i am sitting here alone tonight drinking not-too-bad pinot noir and now it seems that the fire is going at last – there was no kindling and no axe to split the logs and i got pretty angry it being such a cold night and i felt as if i had spoilt something that was good and true and even beautiful often as not but ugly ugly ugly too that dreadful night when i just could not find it within myself to comfort you in your sadness and not only because i perceived myself to be the cause of it but also because of the nightmare of the past which was re-awakened by it – i cannot tell you – it was as if i was back there again in that room with that thin frightened woman that terrible despair and the smell of imminent death

i am full of doubt yes but i am all right – i am complete – i am smooth and mellow and you would have asked too many questions

i didn't want to ask you and i wouldn't have asked you if it was just because i was lonely but i did think that we could comfort each other and to experience some softness together – everything had been so jagged and hard the last few weeks of the depths of that winter

i'd had some ideas about preserving something of myself something precious something that seemed always to be subsumed as soon as i got into bed with a woman and that i was only too happy to part with and something that was almost impossible to regain once it was gone – some part of me didn't want to let go of it this time – i was like a cornered animal but it proved very difficult the more i tried to introduce distance and to keep her at arm's length the more she clung to me until the only option was to push her away as hard as i could and that was sad that was ugly and i suppose that leaves us both with our own peculiar mixture of the sadness of the unobtainable and the unattainable

*it is not about you – there is nothing wrong with you you are great*
*– so what is it then?*
she is frowning
*it is about me – i am …*
*– yes you are post recovery*
*i am* in *recovery … my wounds are real but healing slowly provided*
*they …*

you could say that i should have seen it coming but now i have
to turn her into a character in a story to make sense of it

## three

it had been a strange time: apart from the ferocity of the rain
it was a time when people's brothers mothers and closest
friends were being hacked to death or killed in car crashes
one after the other and their friends and family were left
holding the pieces and to his horror his dreams of blood and
death became real and it created an enormous distance: what
do you say to someone whose mother or brother is hacked to
death?

she seemed to be falling in love with me and i didn't want that
– actually i thought a lot of the love stuff was an implant cul-
turally speaking you know – i thought it was pathological
really falling in love with someone – it seemed to me more
like a symptom of dysfunction and weakness and i didn't want
to share everything with someone anymore – k (you remember her ?) cured me of that one – not in the gentlest of ways
mind you

he says: *i don't want to hurt you but at the same time i don't want*
*to hurt myself … it is terrible what is happening here – i thought*
*everything was clear between us – i thought we had some clarity in*
*what it meant what the implications were … was it you who said in*
*the very beginning that we should keep things light between us*

a character in a story would have paced the room as he would have but he was exhausted: he just sat with his head in his hands his voice barely audible in the darkening room

he says: *you are … it is …. too much for me – i don't want to be that*
*close to anyone*
*he is looking at her intently now*
she says: *don't give me that look*

## epilogue

so she finally came to see me – it was nearly a year and a half later and over that time we were forever running into each other around town without talking or acknowledging each other's presence or existence – she was going back to amer-ica – and it was ok it was good to see her and at least we worked out that we didn't hate each other but as we kept talk-ing and drinking wine and the hours went by i started getting bored and realised there was still plenty of resentment being harboured underneath all of this apparent goodwill and let's-be-friends rhetoric and then after that there was a vast ocean of emptiness with bits of shit floating in it which were uncon-nected with her or any of the united states of america and i was relieved when she finally realised it was time to say good-bye

# Finding the Way Home

## *Alli Barnard*

'Kaz!' Simon yelled when she'd jumped the fence and was close enough to recognise in what was left of the afternoon light. 'What the hell are ya doin' here?'

'Lovely to see you too, Si.' She laughed, crossing the overgrown yard to sit by him on the verandah step.

'Couldn't hack it in the big smoke, eh?' He eyed her worn work clothes, earth-caked boots. She had the same old scruffy blonde hair.

'Nah, back for the shearin'. Don't act too thrilled.'

'I wasn't.' He crinkled his brow in confusion.

'God, Si,' Kassie laughed. 'I was being sarcastic.' She reached over and tried to smooth the wrinkles out on his forehead. He swatted her hand away.

'Don't laugh at me. I ain't stupid. Just cos I ain't doing some fancy degree …'

'Hey,' she interrupted. 'Look at me. Si, look at me. I could never think you're stupid. Never.' Simon looked back at his feet and started shuffling his boots in the dust.

''Member that trap you made for the foxes?' she persisted.

Simon grunted.

'Four in one week, bloody genius.'

'Yeah, I guess.'

'So, what've you been up to?' She settled herself against a post.

'Same's always. Dad's think'n' a' branchin' inta cattle if the season stays good.'

The shadows had well and truly settled into night. A faint silhouette of the surrounding hills the only reminder of the day, and distance.

He got up and flicked on the porch light. 'What the hell's that on ya nose?!'

'It's a nose ring.' She laughed at his expression.

'What the bloody hell'd ya do that for?'

'Fashion, Simon Pike. Have you two met?'

'Talk sense would ya?'

'Sorry.' Her voice lost the frivolity. Their silence was covered by cicada trills, whirring insects and the occasional bleating sheep.

'Happy birthday by the way,' Kassie said.

'Tah.'

'Did you get my letter?'

'Yeah.'

They stared at the dark countryside, moonlight hitting the scraggly gums, the wire along the fence line and bouncing off the ripples in the dam.

'Did you like it?'

She watched him in the porch light, shadows of insects darting across his rough features as they kamikazed into the bare bulb.

'Yeah.'

He wouldn't meet her eye.

'I missed you, Si.'

'Don't sound like it.' He looked at anything, everything but her.

'And what's that supposed to mean?'

'Yer the smart one, you figure it out.'

She looked away but didn't see anything. She smelt the cool, softer air, the grass, the dirt, the lanolin on her skin and clothes. A gum that must have been recently cut down. She was aware of the absence of carbon monoxide, cigarette smoke.

'Smells quieter.'

'Did ya ever make sense?'

She laughed and slapped his leg playfully. He didn't look up but smiled despite himself.

'See, you did miss me.' She smiled.

'Bit, I s'pose.'

'Why are you so mad at me, Si?'

'I ain't.'

'Si …'

'I ain't.'

'Don't try that bullshit with me!'

'Well how else am I s'posed ta be, huh?'

'Just be you!' She was losing the struggle to keep her voice calm.

'I am!'

'No, you're cold.'

'We had a deal.' He was gripping the step so hard his knuckles had turned white.

'What?'

'Malaki. We've bin plannin' it for years. Ya promised.' He turned on her, glaring.

'I was ten!'

'Ya asked.'

She sighed, looking out over the millions of stars. 'Maybe we can still do it – but we've gotta take over the properties before we can combine them, Si. It'll be years yet.'

He didn't reply.

'I am coming back. Believe me, Simon.' She turned his face towards her, looking up at his hurt expression. 'I am,' she whispered. His brown eyes trapped hers for a moment before he turned away. 'I'll see you.' She got up, leaned over, kissed him on the forehead and left.

She walked back across black paddocks. A flyscreen door clattered shut somewhere in the darkness behind her.

# The Hammam

## *Tiffany Barton*

Fatima and I shuffle through the crowds of men with our heads low but still they stare. I can smell hashish, char-grilled peppers, rotting vegetables and my own unwashed odour. We sidestep a steaming pile of donkey shit and Fatima laughs at me gagging. An old woman sits on the side of the road with a pile of lamb offal in front of her, laid out on a clean white sheet. At the meat market we are greeted by rows and rows of sheep's heads, grinning hideously, their tongues rolling obscenely from their mouths. Vendors jostle for space in the crowded street, while donkeys clatter past dragging their dilapidated carts behind them, and men cradle glasses of sweet milky coffee and mint tea at the beverage stands that line the side of the road. The sound of Arabic is everywhere. It's an indiscernible babble, although every now and then a stray word trips in to my understanding. I can count to ten in Arabic now, say hello and thank you, and order vegetables in the market.

There are few women on the street. They go about their business quickly with their heads lowered. I do not meet their eyes anymore. Last week a woman spat at me for wearing the gilebba, their traditional kaftan. We reach the hammam, an old concrete building covered in a mosaic of blue tiles. It is cool and clean inside. An old woman leads us to a wooden bench where we disrobe. We laugh at the difference in each other's bodies. Her swollen breasts with chocolate nipples. Her folds of flesh. My whiteness. My apple breasts. My solid thighs. She tells me the Arabic name for breasts. One is '*bazoola*', two is '*bezezin*'. I laugh at their comic book sound, but they seem more suited to her ample bosom than my insignificant curves.

Inside the sauna there are women everywhere, of all shapes and sizes, washing each other. The older women have tattoos at their brows and temples and henna designs on their hands. There is so much flesh; such roundness and warmth. Their movement is open and sensual, and I am amazed at the free-dom they display, since I know they spend most of their lives concealed in cloth and locked inside.

The hammam is made up of three separate rooms adjoin-ing each other, with varying degrees of heat. The hottest contains copper pipes that burn to touch and basins of cool water that create the steam. We choose the second room which smoulders enough to make the sweat run rivers down our skin, but is not as hot as the first room, where even breathing requires the most intense effort. We sit on rubber mats and Fatima produces a small slippery ball like fine liquorice mud which she rubs into my skin. I do the same to her and we wait for the steam to draw the dirt and sweat from our bodies. Fatima takes a rough cloth and scrubs my flesh hard, so that the dirt and dead skin form in little balls on my belly, back and arms. She takes her hair down and laughs to see so much dirt on me. I don't think she was expecting this from a white girl. Her face shows a flushed sensuality I have not seen before. Strands of hair catch in her mouth. My skin is almost scrubbed raw: I have never felt so clean.

When we get back to her family home Abi laughs at my flushed clean glow. He tickles my face like he would a small child.

'Did they tell you their secrets?' he asks.

'A few.'

'Tell me.'

'But then they wouldn't be secret, would they?'

'It's been so long since I went there. I got thrown out when I was six for holding my penis and staring at a woman's breasts. After that I had to go with my father and watch the men jerking off. I used to cry and beg my mother to take me but she said I was too old.'

'Poor baby.'

He slaps my behind and chases me upstairs. In our room we kiss and wrestle and fuck. We try to repress our screams but he never can. I think sex is the only way he can let out all his frustration and anger, and he must have a lot of it because ever since we arrived in his country all he wants to do is fuck. We come together and he screams like a dying animal. I cringe, wondering what his parents must think. Afterwards he withdraws from me quickly and wipes himself, handing me tissues without meeting my eyes. He always does this and it always makes me ashamed. I think he mustn't like my smell, even though he obviously enjoys fucking me. I say nothing as usual and we go downstairs for dinner. I worry that his family will smell me too, and I try to keep my thighs pressed together throughout the meal.

Fatima grins at me cheekily and points to a piece of zucchini.

'*Latifa smeeto?*' she enquires, meaning 'What's this?'

'Zucchini,' I reply in mock innocence. Everyone covers their mouths trying not to laugh except for the father who frowns. '*Zucchi*' effectively means 'backside' in Moroccan Arabic. I found this out earlier when I helped to prepare the meal and we were teaching each other the name of vegetables in Arabic and English. Now I pretend not to know why they're so shocked and I secretly wink at Fatima. 'You are a devil,' says Abi and I poke out my tongue at him. It's my eighteenth birthday in two days time. I wonder if he'll remember.

That night Abi's friend Mustafa comes over and we smoke hashish on the roof. I have one puff and I'm delirious, staring out at the rooftops, listening to the Koran being wailed from a tinny loudspeaker at a nearby mosque. I look down at the donkeys and carts and watch people and rats scurrying in the streets. I feel omnipresent as I imagine the insides of the houses where the old women bend five times to Mecca on their prayer mats, the girls practise belly dancing behind closed doors, and the men hold hands in the streets or silently pass their kif pipes to their brothers. I feel all-seeing and insignificant at the same time as I listen to Abi and Mustafa speak in their thick language, which washes over me like an exotic song but excludes me and leaves me feeling lonely in the darkness. I wonder what they're saying about me, what they all think of me really. Does Abi tell his friends what it's like to fuck a white girl? Do they hate me because I'm easy? Do they desire me? Are his sisters scared because they like me, and what will it do to their reputation, being associated with a loose white woman? My head reels and the night heat is dense upon my skin. The stars seem heavy in the sky and my eyeballs sit like lead in their sockets, my jaw slack and loose, my mouth dry.

Abi's mother is sick. Something in her stomach. She's been this way for a while but it seems to be getting worse. She barely eats, perhaps a bit of bread or apple. From time to time she looks at me hopefully as if I might produce some miracle to cure her, but all I have is my camera, my inappropriate clothes, my bad command of the language and my naivety. I smile ineptly at her and ask her how she is. She always shakes her head sadly.

Abi gets enraged sometimes. It began on the ferry over. This tension. I could see the stiffness in his body, and as soon as he set foot in his country he began to fight. He fought anyone who rubbed him up the wrong way. It was Ramadan when we arrived. No eating, drinking, smoking or sex before sunset. He ate and smoked openly and kissed me passionately in public. It enraged the old women who saw us. They shot me deathly looks and screamed at him. He seemed to really enjoy fighting with them. 'This isn't my country anymore,' he told them. 'I am not Moroccan, I am not a Muslim.' But at some point the anger turned. He began to lash out at me. He couldn't stand his family's misery, the way they all looked to him for help. He began to hate me for my sense of freedom and privilege.

Once he walked in while I was playing dress-ups with his sisters. I was showing them my new bikini, trying to undulate my belly while they laughed. One of them was wearing my miniskirt with knee-high boots. She blushed when she saw him and quickly covered herself with her gilebba. He asked them to leave the room.

'You are a spoilt slutty white girl. You drink alcohol, you smoke cigarettes and hashish like a man, you show your body, you swear, you slept with other men before me, but my sisters will probably die virgins. Who will marry them? They have no money. You have no idea, do you? You and your cultural imperialism, your washing machine, your hair dryer and your American bullshit TV. Your culture is a whore. You women are all sluts and your men are idiots. You think it's funny giving my sisters your clothes? Teaching them Western dances? Making them laugh in public? You make them think they have a chance at something better. You are the devil. I should kick you out of my house. You have no right to be here. Get out of my sight. I have no energy for you anymore. You drain me.'

I didn't know how to respond. At home I would have walked away from him, to the comfort of my family and friends, but I was sure if we were back in Australia he wouldn't talk to me in this way. My need to survive in his country was greater than my need to defend myself. I said I was sorry and tried to hold his hand. He pushed me away and stormed out to smoke kif with his friends. I wiped my face and joined his sisters in the kitchen. I didn't tell them what he said. We kneaded dough for the next day's bread and taught each other our language.

I learnt to say 'I like you very much.' I tried to forget the things he said. Tomorrow would be better.

He doesn't wish me a happy birthday. We catch a train to Fez and sometime that night I quietly remind him. He waves it away, 'We don't celebrate birthdays here. There are more important things.' I try not to get upset, but that night when he leaves me to go and smoke hashish I think of my family and friends. Homesickness washes over me in thick sticky waves.

The next day we visit the old town with his cousin Muhammad. At the gates a donkey tries to mount another, his penis huge and erect. Hundreds of boys gather to laugh and throw stones at the poor beast. Muhammad leads us down alleyways so narrow we have to flatten ourselves against a wall when a donkey and cart pass by. We move into the labyrinth that is central Fez, through dark tunnels and passageways until we reach the small concrete room where Abi's aunt Layla has lived since her husband died. She has a few cushions, a rug, some blankets, a gas stove and some pots and pans. She gave her husband no children and so he gave everything to his other wife. She hugs Abi and I take a photo of them both smiling. We exchange a few words. I wonder what she thinks of me. Does she resent me too the way he does? I suddenly feel guilty, to have such freedom and privilege. I am in the centre of this lost world with this lonely woman who smiles and sits placidly with her hands in her lap and I want to go home. I silently berate myself for being so mournful. Her hardships are a hundred times worse than mine.

When we get back from Fez, Fatima and Miriam greet me with wide smiles. I go upstairs and share my shopping bounty with them. A Berber scarf, silver jewellery, black kohl, some drums and men's sandals. They laugh when they see these and call me Abdullah. I like these shoes better than the ladies' sandals which are uncomfortable and impractical for walking. I shuffle around in them and act like a man while they squeal with delight. '*Willie, willie, willie,*' they say, which has the same meaning as 'Ooh la la'. Fatima and I tie scarves around our waist and Miriam drums while we belly dance. I stick some socks down my pants and thrust at Fatima with my groin, grinning and dribbling lasciviously at her. She acts coy then shies away from me and beckons seductively. I move towards her thrusting my hips lewdly. Miriam has gone red with embarrassment and hilarity. She keeps checking the door to make sure no one is there. I dance over to her and wiggle my hips in her face. She's almost choking with repressed laughter. I open my shirt and shake my breasts, wiggling my eyebrows suggestively. There's a knock at the door. I look at the girls, whose faces have suddenly drained of colour. I fix up my clothes and open the door. It's their father, Hassan. He looks sternly at the girls and speaks in Arabic. I can't understand what he's saying. After he leaves they sit quietly, not meeting my eye. I start wiggling again and in a hoarse voice call to them, 'Fatima, Miriam, what did he say?' They still sit quietly.

'Faatimaa, Miiriaam, what did he say?' They press their hands to their mouths and begin to snort. I wiggle over to them and tickle them all over, 'Faatimaa! Miiriaam!! What did he say??' Still they laugh into their hands and cry for me to stop. Abi bursts in and laughs to see us crying and weak with humour. But when we have calmed down he whispers into my ear, 'My father says you will turn them into whores.' I draw in my breath and look at them. They know what we're talking about, and they stare down at the floor. My skin prickles with heat. 'I'm sorry,' I whisper, and I leave, closing the door behind me.

One afternoon I sit with Fatima and Miriam on the rooftop while everyone else sleeps. Miriam sighs and I ask her what's wrong. '*La vie*,' she replies. Fatima echoes her in an almost silent voice, '*La vie*.'

We are nearing the end of our visit. Abi is desperate to do something for his family. He asks me if I'll consider marrying one of his brothers to give him residency in Australia. I ask him how many donkeys I'll receive. He thumps me on the knee. 'No respect,' he says. 'You white women hate yourselves.'

I do not reply.

It's time to leave. Abi has work to return to in Australia and I'll rejoin my family in France. We're catching a train to Tangiers and a ferry to Algeciras in Spain. Everyone gathers in the living room. Hassan and I shake hands and touch our hearts, '*Bslama. Salaam aleykum.*'

'*Aleykum salaam.*'

His mother holds me and whispers to me to take care of her son. I embrace her frailty as gently as I can. Her sister and niece hold me with tears in their eyes. I shake hands with his brothers who show polite affection for me. Finally I come to Fatima and Miriam. I gulp in air and hold them tightly to me. They begin to wail. We clutch at each other. I hold back the tears, knowing they'll be too loud, too much of an embarrassment. Fatima whispers, 'We don't care if Abi never comes back, but we want to see you again.' She says it desperately, looking searchingly into my eyes. I nod, knowing now that I'm more powerless than ever. I feel I can never match what they've given me – they've shown me unconditional love and affection – more than their brother ever could. I had no idea the bond between women could be this deep. Abi draws me away. I can't stand to look at their weeping faces. On the train I sob and sob. Abi holds me with warmth. At least I can share some of his pain. The dry miles pass and the distance wells up.

# Like a Christmas Cake

*Creed O'Hanlon*

She wakes in darkness, shivering, a sudden chill on her back like the breath of a ghost. She lies still, eyes closed in a pretence of sleep, as he slides from beneath the *kake-buton* to rise and pad across the *tatami* flooring to the bathroom. Fragile walls mute the sibilant sputter of the shower and the rubbery squeak of bare feet.

She reaches under her pillow to retrieve a small mobile phone. Drawing the *kake-buton* up over her head, she glances at a graphic of an analogue clock glowing on the *keitai*'s colour screen – 5.11 a.m. In exactly thirty-nine minutes, he will catch the subway to his office in Shinagawa. She replaces the *keitai* under the pillow and turns on her side, folding her legs up almost to her chest, like a foetus within a dark cotton womb. Just a few shallow breaths and she is at the edge of unconsciousness. She does not hear him leave.

She wakes again, two hours later, in a watery sunlight diffused by a wide, bleached cotton blind, like a photographer's scrim, drawn down over the window. Bleary-eyed, she stretches across the futon to the floor for a pack of Kools and a disposable lighter. After fumbling to extract the last cigarette with her long fingernails, she lights it and sucks the smoke deep into her lungs until it burns. For a brief moment, her mind is as empty and emotionless as a monk's during *zazen*. She is ageless, no longer subject to space or time.

Tomorrow is her twenty-ninth birthday.

She has to go to the toilet. Prone, she pulls on a Moschino T-shirt, which smells of stale menthol, and a pair of knickers she finds crumpled between her feet. Even with the blinds down, she is self-conscious about moving around the apartment naked. She hasn't always felt this way. She can remember with explicit tactility the slim body she had more than a decade ago. As a *kogyaru*, a precocious girl in her last year of high school, she lived on a diet of miso soup, *natto* and cigarettes pilfered from her father, and she wasn't afraid to show off her long, brown limbs and torso, even when she travelled to Tokyo from her family's home in the hive-like tenements of Saitama, braving the leering, middle-aged perverts, or *chikan*, who tried to molest her among the crush of commuters on the Saikyo line.

She sheds her soiled clothes in front of a mirror in the windowless bathroom, and surveys her body with forensic detachment. It is still brown and thin but to her eyes, it looks, somehow, amorphous. She pokes the unblemished skin on her arms and legs to test its tautness, and pinches her narrow hips and concave pelvis to check for fat. Her palms heft her small breasts and flat buttocks to gauge their subsidence, and her fingertips trace the shallow fissures at the corners of her eyes' epicanthic folds. Like many Japanese, her lower front teeth are crooked, yellowed by nicotine. She pretends a smile that exposes only the straighter, less damaged enamel of her upper teeth and reminds herself to visit a dentist.

Her body is the only object of the few disordered rituals she observes. As a child, her grandmother took her to the local public baths and, with an almost spiritual rigour, ensured that she learned not only to bathe with an abrasive efficiency but to look no further than the surface of things, to respect the efficacy of veneer. It was always implicit that her appearance was an asset, and even before she could possibly understand why, she was encouraged to put every effort into improving its longevity and value – a value to be determined later, by others, most of them men.

She still senses her grandmother's stern grey eyes every time she bathes. If she were still alive, she would be fretting about her grand-daughter who had failed – she would use that word with bitterness – to find a husband by the time she was twenty-five. Marriage for her grandmother's and mother's generations was not about love; it was a practical transaction in which a husband provided a reasonable level of security, comfort and status and, in return, a dutiful wife raised their children, cooked, cleaned and, from time to time, serviced his sexual needs. Affection was a happy accident, not a necessary part of the deal.

'My dear Naoko, a man needs just four things from a woman,' her grandmother once told her. 'And not necessarily from the same woman.'

It is not so different now. All the girls with whom she graduated from high school in Saitama are married. And yet, as far as she can tell, their husbands are strangers to them. Junior *salariman* at large banks, manufacturing and trading companies, they leave home early in the morning and return late at night, six days a week, and if they are busy or they are trying to impress their managers, they sleep at their offices and do not come home for a couple of days. Bound more to their corporate cultures than to their families, their wives' forbearance is still no less than they expect.

She lives alone, in a studio apartment in the fashionable Tokyo neigbourhood of Hiroo. She is well paid as an account associate for a large advertising agency. The women she grew up with feel sorry for her.

'I met someone interesting yesterday.'

Naoko is sunk deep into the soft cushions of an armchair upholstered with scuffed crimson velvet on the second floor of a Starbucks in Roppongi, sipping a warm caramel latte grande from a white china mug. Next to her, a slight but animated woman in low-cut Diesel cargo pants and an MTV T-shirt is sitting sideways in a semi-lotus position on an identical armchair: Eri is twenty-one and she works as a secretary at the agency.

Eri says nothing. *It must be a man,* she thinks. *Japanese women are never interesting to each other.*

A wide window in front of them overlooks a grimy street lined with restaurants, nightclubs and bars with broken-English names. At any other hour, the whole district would be teeming with people; now, there are only street cleaners and a couple of pretty hostesses in satin evening gowns staggering towards the open door of a taxi.

'I was at Shin Hiroo Park,' Naoko goes on. 'I sometimes go there early in the morning to walk before heading to the office. Anyway, there was this guy ...'

*I knew it.*

'And he was walking one of those liver-coloured dogs, what are they called?'

'Weimaraners.'

'Yeah. Anyway, I went over and asked if I could pat it. He didn't speak Japanese very well but ...'

'Wait a minute. He was a *gaijin?*'

'Yeah. English, I think. He was very pale.'

'Do you speak English?'

'Ve-ery lit-tle,' Naoko says in halting English, each syllable sounded with the light percussive attack of Japanese. Both women giggle but only the older woman raises her hand to her mouth in a reflex of traditional etiquette.

'So how do you know he's interesting?'

'He directs music videos. I think he's pretty successful because he drives a BMW. He invited me to a party tonight, some sort of launch for a new record label.'

'Oh, I think I'm going to that. It's at that new restaurant, the one with the roof garden, in Shibuya,' Eri says. After a slight pause, she asks: 'Are you going to tell your boyfriend?'

It is strange to hear him referred to as her 'boyfriend'. She has been seeing him for three years and they sleep together at her place once or twice a week, usually on a Saturday night or when he has to work late at the office, but whatever it is they share is tenuous, fragmented, like so many of the relationships Japanese women of her age have.

'No,' she said. *Should I?*

'Have you ever dated a *gaijin?*'

'I'm not dating this guy. He's invited to me a party, that's all.'

'But have you?'

'No. They scare me a little.'

'Really?' Her friend is surprised 'My mother calls me *gaijin-zuki.* I've been with a few.'

Naoko can't work out whether she is amused or shocked. Seeing her friend's eyes widen, Eri giggles. 'You haven't thought about it?' Eri asks. 'I mean, how long have you been waiting for this guy you're with to ask you to marry him?'

Naoko had hoped that he might ask in the first year they were together, not because she loved him, she didn't, but because she was, and still is in many ways, no different from her friends: she wants to be a wife, she wants to take her place in the traditional scheme of things, she wants to make her parents happy. Now she is inured to the probability that he will leave for someone younger, prettier and less independent – someone, in other words, a little more pliable. He is thirty-two, a mid-level manager in one of the unglamorous divisions of Sony, and he still lives with his parents in Setagaya. She won't miss him; he is hardly around as it is.

'My mother used to tell me that a Japanese woman is *kurisumasu keiki no you*, like a Christmas cake,' Eri says. 'On the twenty-third it's on display, on the twenty-fourth it's still fresh, but if it isn't eaten on the twenty-fifth it will go stale.'

'Oh, thanks,' Naoko says, holding her mug closer to her face with both hands to hide her embarrassment. 'I hadn't really thought of myself as a bit of dry cake!' But the truth is, she had, sort of: lying alone in the darkness, late at night, she sometimes imagined her body beset by a creeping desiccation – the blood in her arteries granulating, her skin flaking like torn strips of rice paper – as the reservoir of her youth evaporates.

'That's the thing,' her friend tells her. 'Looking at you, a *gaijin* doesn't see an older woman ...'

'I am not old!'

'OK. But even Japanese of your age are like a dream to them. You're thin, your skin's still smooth. Their women diet and exercise and spend a fortune on cosmetics to get what we come by naturally.'

*Just as we dye our hair every colour except black and wear shoes with high heels or elevated soles to make us look taller, more Western,* Naoko thinks. She looks around at the early morning customers nursing their coffees, muffins, cinnamon rolls and curried chicken salad sandwiches. There are several tables of young 'office ladies', or *OLs*, like them but dressed to suit more conservative office codes, and here and there, grey-suited *salariman* asleep, their chins resting on their chests as if they have been garrotted by their dull, patterned ties. There are weary students with laptops, books and coffee-stained papers strewn across the tables, and half-sober hostesses, their heads resting on the shoulders of young, black-suited club touts with bleached blond hair and artificial tans. There are several foreigners of various races; none of them looks like a tourist.

'Would you marry a *gaijin*?' she asks Eri.

'No,' Eri says. She thinks about it for a moment, then adds, 'No. My mum would never forgive me. And a lot of these guys have been married before and have had kids. I'm still young, I want to find someone who is ...'

'Fresh?' Naoko asks, with an acerbity that startles them both. It compels a mortified silence between them. Unable to apologise, as she knows she should, Naoko drops her head back and closes her eyes. *Is it possible to be worn out by your own culture?* Ray Charles is singing The Beatles' 'Yesterday'. In a voiceless karaoke, she mouths an approximation of the words; by the second chorus she is lost in the poignancy of her own unheard performance.

She ascends into night from the subterranean maze of Shibuya station. Crowds of late-shift commuters and youthful shoppers intermingle in the turbulent human river that spills across the crosswalks beneath the glow of huge, animated plasma screens, coloured neon ascending the facades of every structure, and billboards lit with bright halogen. On the concrete plaza that forms one corner of Shibuya Crossing, you can sense as much as hear the subsonic rumble of congested traffic, of trains beneath the ground and overhead, of indecipherable snatches of music and of voice-overs reverberating from the giant screens, and of the subdued stir of half a million individuals swarming the narrow pavements. This is the Tokyo of cliché, the Tokyo that everyone who does not live here has in his or her head, but it is no less real and impressive for that.

A large group of errant high-school girls is perched on the steps in front of the brushed-steel and opaque-glass structure of her destination. Smoking, chatting, raising delicate hands to their mouths as they trade girlish confidences, they are still dressed in their blue, faux-sailor uniforms, thick white leg warmers bunched around their lower calves and pleated skirts rolled at the waist to pull the hems up to their thighs. There is an unnerving sexual energy among them and she wonders whether they are aware of it and whether it was the same when she was their age.

*Probably*, she thinks. *Japanese girls are taught early to use their youth while they have it, as if it is all they will ever have.* Some of them, too many, will trade it in *enjo kosai*, or 'compensated interaction', with middle-aged *salariman*.

The elevator ascends two dozen floors in as many seconds to open onto a dim, cavernous room. At the room's centre, lasers weave flickering blue and green filaments into Hindi-looking *katakana* symbols above an indistinct mass heaving in time to a bass-laden Bhangra beat. Around the edge of the room are booths, all of them filled with small parties within the main party, and long tables on which are arrayed glasses of champagne and elaborate sushi. Waiters in black slacks and T-shirts bear large silver trays with an almost balletic agility through the guests milling at the edge of the dance floor.

She sees neither the Englishman nor Eri, nor does she recognise anyone, except a few of the B-list *idoru* and their handlers who always turn up at these events for the photo opportunities. Hesitantly, she moves further into the room. She has made a mistake with her choice of a short, black Calvin Klein cocktail dress and high-heel, strapless Guccis. She had wanted to elongate her legs beneath the narrow A-line of the dress but now she has to shift her weight from one leg to the other to relieve the ache in her calves. She accepts a glass of champagne from a passing waiter and gulps half of it to dull the pain. She threads her way to the other side of the room, where the booths appear to be occupied by more *gaijin*.

Coarse fingers grip her upper arm.

'Hey, do you speak English?' He is a large, plump Westerner in a tailored, grey business suit, his long grey hair pulled back into a scraggly ponytail. He smells of whisky.

*He must be in the advertising business.*

She gives him a wan smile and holding one hand up, palm towards him in a polite gesture to stop, tries to pull away from him. His grip tightens.

'Come on, join us.' He offers her a crooked grin that he thinks is charming.

'No. Please,' she insists in English. Frightened now, she yanks her arm away and stumbles towards the protective throng of the dance floor. She penetrates its dim jostle far enough to become invisible to him and stops. Unsure of what she should do next – *it's impossible to dance in these shoes* – she checks her *keitai* in case Eri has left her a message. The screen shows four missed calls, all from a familiar Sony extension, but no voicemail.

Nearby, a cluster of frenetic young girls are bouncing in place on their toes; they scream with delight as a bright strobe turns the images on their colourful Bathing Ape and Hysteric Glamour T-shirts into a dizzyingly hyperkinetic cartoon.

All she recalls of the rest of the evening are shards of disorienting incident.

She is sitting in a chest-high tub of steaming, sandalwood-fragranced water, a rolled handtowel beneath her neck, her head lolling against the reinforced plastic wall. A cigarette dangles from between her fingers and a glass of wine is alongside the tub on the floor. She is not drunk but she is light-headed enough to enjoy the amniotic weightlessness, the seeming absence of substance that momentarily lets her mind float free.

*I drank too much.*

*I got tired of the music's visceral din.*

*A spiral staircase ascended to the roof garden.*

*I found the Englishman there, sprawled on a daybed beneath the stars.*

*Eri and another girl were with him.*

*I watched in the darkness as he kissed the girl and Eri unzipped his orange Prada trousers.*

She feels nothing, in as much as she had expected nothing, the residue of a rationality that, her grandmother used to tell her, was a racial trait, although in her grandmother's case, it was tempered by petty superstitions and ancient rituals for luck. Certainly, she feels nothing for the Englishman. And yet she also feels nothing as a disconcerting mindlessness, a careless void. Maybe she really is past her use-by date; maybe this is how it feels when youth slips away.

She reaches for the glass on the floor and takes a small sip from it. She takes a drag from the cigarette and exhales the smoke in a long weary sigh. Not long now before midnight.

Tomorrow is her twenty-ninth birthday.

# Siege

## *Amra Pajalic*

**September 1992**

**1.**

We are in Ramo's cellar. It seems nearly the whole street is here. We have been here for three weeks now. I think today is 8 September. The days blur into each other as we wait, so I have to number my diary entries. Sometimes we go for two days without water or a toilet or food.

I am repulsed by our combined smells. The smell of fear, the smell of the slop bucket hidden by a strung-up blanket in the corner, the stench of our unwashed bodies.

We all take turns crouching behind the blanket and then going upstairs to empty our slop out the window. At first we used to avert our eyes when someone made their way to the corner. Now the combined sounds blend in.

The sound of piss trickling into the bucket, or shit dropping down to splatter onto the smelly leftovers from previous visitors. The sound of grenades and bullets wreaking destruction outside. Sometimes it sounds like a rocket-propelled grenade is right over us, that we should expect the roof to cave in on us and crush us to death.

But that is another thing we have gotten used to. We don't flinch anymore when a grenade whistles overhead.

**2.**

I haven't seen Darko for a month.

The last time I saw him was at the hospital where he works translating for UNPROFOR. He told me he was going to try to get out through them. He plans on going to Novi Sad where his brother is and then onto Slovenia where he has other family.

He asked me to go with him. I didn't answer him.

We went to his house and made love with frantic desperation. The desperation of not knowing if we would see each other again. For a while our differences were forgotten, the hurtful words we exchanged that day were soothed with our touches and kisses.

Before I left, he asked me again if I would come with him. I looked into his eyes. My first love, my lover of seven years. He knows me, he knows the fear I carry. I could see the hurt I had caused him, and still I couldn't tell him. I couldn't give him the words he needed.

**3.**

Nermin received the draft today. He is just seventeen years old but they are calling him up. My baby brother has to go to the army. He hasn't even had the chance to finish high school. He doesn't know anything about weapons or fighting.

He ran away from the house, we know that he was crying. He came back with red-rimmed eyes hours later. After Nermin left Mum started crying too. Father tried to comfort her, but he was trying to hold in his own fear. He left and hid out in the garage for the rest of the day. Ferida and I sat with Mum on the couch, our arms around each other as we sobbed quietly.

I wrote a letter to Faruk. I tried not to worry him and make him feel guilty about leaving, but I had to tell him about Nermin being drafted. It's not his fault that he got out and Nermin stayed. We didn't know what would happen. When Nermin started crying and clutching Mum, our parents let him stay and forced Faruk to leave by himself. Faruk was the oldest and had to be protected. We didn't know that in only two years' time they would be drafting any male up to the job.

**4.**

We haven't received any humanitarian aid for two weeks. It's getting scary. There is no minced beef, or potato, or cheese, or spinach to make pita. There is nothing but rice. We have now learnt to make pita by mixing rice with powdered milk and vinegar and leaving it to ferment overnight. This is our substitute for cheese. Instead of spinach we use beetroot leaves. Now we just need to find a substitute for minced beef.

Father goes to town every day to exchange what little vegetables we have for food. Between giving out onions to the neighbours and the thieves stealing from the garden, there isn't much left.

I'm worried about Darko. It's worse in the city, they have no backyards where they can grow vegetables and are starving. We have heard that people are committing suicide.

The aid stopped when during shootings at the airport, a bullet hit the tail of the plane in which Phillip Morion, the General of United Nations, was flying.

Who are they punishing?

**October 1992**

**1.**

I wrote another letter to Faruk in Austria and sent it through the Red Cross. We're all worried about him, we're worried that he might try to return like so many others did. He can help us more by being outside, rather than being trapped here like we are.

The water truck hasn't come for a while to deliver water. We heard that there is no petrol to power them. Father has been going at night to get water from the well at Ismana's house.

Every time he leaves the house, we wonder if he will make it back. Although it is safer at night, we're still scared.

## 2.

Darko called today. He was going to meet a food convoy. He didn't say it, but I know he will be trying to get out. He said that he would call. I pray he makes it.

Ramo's cellar was getting too crowded and the cold of winter is starting. We are now in our house. We hide in the small toilet under the stairs when the shelling starts.

We mostly stay in what was Ferida's room. We have put bags of sand nearly to the top of the window, blocking out bullets and sunshine. We can't leave the house because it's too dangerous so we are stuck in this one dark room with each other for company.

We play cards to keep ourselves amused. Ferida is becoming a regular card shark when she can tear herself away from her textbooks. She is still studying for her exams. I guess it at least gives her something to do. Although I wonder if it's futile, if they will hold the exams at all.

I am studying from my German and English books. As a refugee it would be good to know another language.

We irritate each other in this small space.

Father has the radio on all day. We have used up all the batteries we had, first the batteries from the remote, then the calculator, then we boiled and re-boiled them all. Now the boiling of batteries doesn't work anymore. We got the battery from the car and are trying to ration our listening.

Once that is finished, we will be cut off from outside news. Although who knows, that might be better than listening to the lies. At least Zagreb Radio lies less than Serbia Radio.

Since winter started we wash our hair in a bowl and bathe once a month. We have some firewood left from summer, but there isn't enough to last the whole five months of winter. We were forced to use our supplies to cook in summer because there was no electricity.

According to the official news on the radio there is no

artillery action. UNPROFOR only record grenades sized 150 millimetres and up. I guess snipers and heavy machine-gun fire aren't worth recording. It's not as if they can kill us.

## 3.

Mum is sick. Nermin comes home for seventy-two hours and then goes again for forty-eight hours as a lookout. She watches him with frantic eyes. When Nermin leaves she can't sleep and watches the door frantically, waiting.

When he comes home, she clutches at him. She isn't eating much. She puts her share of the food aside and tries to share it among us. But she saves the most for Nermin.

He is changing. I can see it in his eyes. He took the Metallica emblems off his jacket so Mum could sew on the Bosnian's army emblem, the Golden Ljiljan. He's started carrying the Koran with him, and he was the one who was the least religious of all of us. We are scared to ask him about what he sees.

They are talking about negotiations on the radio. But it's all a lie. Negotiations or no, we are still getting bombed every day. After every negotiation ends, or a cease-fire, they bomb us even more ferociously.

## 4.

In the city all the trees are cut. People are now reduced to pulling out stumps to try and collect firewood for winter. Everything looks so bare.

They said on the radio, 'Sarajevo trees are dying so that people can survive.'

They have run out of burial room at the Lion's cemetery. Now they are burying people in the athletic track at the stadium. I guess Sarajevo will always have its fame. Once it was for the Winter Olympics of 1984, now it is for the war of the Balkans. I guess the dead will provide company for the ghosts of the Olympics.

They can't hold burials during the day. We provide easy targets for snipers. Now all burials take place at night.

## November 1992

**1.**
Joke from the radio:
  Do you know the motto for the Serbian Pacifist Party?
  Serbia all the way to the Pacific.

**2.**
We heard through the grapevine that they are distributing
help again. Ferida and I went to the city. Snipers were in good
form. It took us three hours to make a trip that took twenty
minutes in peacetime. It was worth it. Each member in the
household received: 300 grams soy flour, 500 grams corn
flour, half a litre of oil, one soap for clothes, tin of fish 400
grams, tin of beef 450 grams.

**3.**
We sent another letter to Faruk. This is the third letter we've
sent. So many others have received responses from family
members outside of the country. Our biggest fear is that he
has tried to return. This time we sent it through the ADEH
French humanitarian organisation.
  I can't try to call Darko's friends and see if he made it
through. I've been sending letters but I don't know if they will
arrive.
  In the letter to Faruk I wrote the phone numbers of
Darko's friends. I'm hoping Faruk will be able to call them
and find out where Darko is.

**4.**
I dreamt about Darko again last night. It was the night he
asked me to marry him. In my dream I said yes. His face lit
up with joy.
  He said to me, 'Bahra, I will always love you.'
  Then I woke up.

## December 1992

**1.**

We have had two weeks of peace. The sun is shining, the kitchen is redolent with tasty smells as Mum bakes, and cooks, and bakes. The luxury of sitting down at a table and eating dinner like a normal family cannot be equalled. For a few minutes we are human beings, not bottles lined up for target practice.

Father fell off the roof. He's OK but he hurt his hip. He was up fixing the last of the artillery damage. Soothing the cracks on the rent surface like a father soothing his child. It took him twenty years to build this house, a brick at a time.

It should not matter so much, a house compared to a limb or a life. But it does.

**2.**

They've started again.

**3.**

I think about what would have happened if I had said yes. Would I be here now? As Darko's wife I would have been able to get out with him. My family would have been unhappy, but now, with the war, it all becomes unimportant.

I wrote to him. I told him I was sorry I let fear get the best of me. That I was too scared of what my family and friends thought. After I wrote the letter, I placed it on the fire.

**4.**

It's New Year in a few minutes. I wish for Darko to be safe and happy, even if it is without me. I wish for Faruk to be well. I wish the war will end soon and everyone will be OK.

I wish I will see Darko again.

## January 1993

### 1.

I haven't heard from Darko for three months now. I am hoping that he got through the blockade, that he is some place where he doesn't fear daily for his life.

It's hard not knowing. Chances are if he didn't make it, I will never find out. He will become just another body that litters the countryside.

We haven't had coffee for five months. We grind the rice we get from humanitarian aid and pretend it is real coffee. I can't remember the taste anymore.

### 2.

Ferida and I returned from the city. We went to where the supermarket used to be, they are now distributing humanitarian aid there. We used to go there to buy food, now we go to beg.

I don't know what's worse. To be hit by a bomb or a sniper, a sniper or a bomb. I guess if I could choose I would rather a sniper's bullet to the brain.

But that doesn't happen very often. They hit Nermana down the street. The bullet ricocheted inside of her and went through her intestines. She has a bag attached to her stomach and is fed through an IV tube.

Ferida has completed two exams for school. She got an eight for Anatomy and nine for Sociology, so she can enrol in her third year. We still don't know if school will be held. Her eyes are hurting from studying by candlelight in the shelter. She will probably need glasses when this finishes.

### 3.

Father went to the market yesterday to exchange the cigarettes that Nermin gets as payment from the army. He overheard a conversation between two black marketeers. They were saying they had a shipment of coffee but were putting the bags aside in order to make more of a profit later on.

Father attacked them, told them they should be ashamed about exploiting people in these times. One of them pointed to the gun under his jacket and told Father to get lost.

He's hidden in the garage now. Mum is praying. I didn't think she knew how.

**4.**

Last night I dreamt I was in Kogo, before the war. I was sitting at our table flipping through *Bravo* magazine. Darko was late as usual so I was catching up on the Hollywood gossip and reading hair and make-up tips. I was staring at a picture of a girl with dark glossy hair styled into a cascade of curls. There were instructions next to the picture about how to replicate the style. I was thinking about how I wanted to buy the brush and styling gel and how Ferida and I would practise doing my hair.

The waitress brought my coffee and placed it in front of me, her hands carefully setting the cup on the table near the edge of my magazine. I didn't look up as she walked away. I reached out and curled my hands around the coffee cup. I lifted the cup to my lips, smelling the dark, heavy scent. The smell hit the back of my throat, making my tastebuds crave the bitter-sweet taste in my mouth. I tilted the cup against my lips. The smooth, warm texture slid onto my tongue. And then I swallowed.

**February 1993**

**1.**

Father spoke to me about Darko today. He asked if I had heard from him. I told him no.

I remember the last time Father mentioned Darko. It was three years ago when he answered the phone and Darko asked for me. He hung up on him and told me that he would never accept a Serbian in his house.

Father told me not to worry. That he could have still made it and just hasn't had the chance to answer my letters.

**2.**

We are running low on supplies. Father doesn't feel well so it will be up to me and Ferida to go to the market to exchange the vegetables. I hate the thought of it. Father wouldn't let us go the few times we offered because it's so dangerous.

He's still hoping he will feel better.

**3.**

Faruk wrote to us today. He said that he received all our letters and replied each time. He called Darko's friends. They haven't heard from him.

My heart broke. I know now that it is futile.

He is gone.

## LIBERATION NEWSPAPER
## OBITUARY

### *23 February 1993*

With deep regret the Osmanagic family announces to our family and friends that our beloved daughter and sister Bahra Osmanagic was shot and killed by sniper on 22 February 1993 in Sarajevo, aged twenty-six years.

She will be remembered by her bereaved parents Hanija and Saban Osmanagic, and her siblings Faruk, Ferida and Nermin.

The funeral is to be held near Olympic Hall Zetra at 10 p.m. tomorrow night.

# The Conversion

## *Carla Sari*

'I've got a visitor from Australia,' Leda said. 'Why don't you come and meet her? She's nineteen, just three years older than you. She's fluent in Italian and her name's Thea.' Leda pronounced Thea without the *th* sound.

I'd been watching a TV program called *Passaporto* and picked up expressions like, Thank you, This is my thumb and Thursday is the fifth day of the week. I, too, had found the *th*s hard to handle.

Leda, my great-aunt, often had foreign visitors. She lived in a flat close to the train station in Venice. I arrived at her place the following day.

'Is that you, Anna? Come in. Thea's stepped out to get some milk. She came loaded up with cereals.' Leda pointed to three boxes of cornflakes lined up on the kitchen bench.

'Didn't she know you can buy them here?'

'She'll soon find out. Make sure you say her name correctly. It's Thea Thurgood. You have to put the tip of your tongue under your front teeth. Like this. She made me repeat her name till I got it right.' Leda's eyes shone with amusement. 'Sit down, dear. What's wrong? Why are you nervous?'

'I'm not nervous,' I replied, assuming a relaxed pose. 'Is she here on holidays?'

'She's here for the Bellini exhibition and to collect some material for her father who's an art historian. She's having a bit of a holiday as well. It's her first visit to Italy. I'm sure you'll like her.'

'What religion is she?' I asked.

Leda frowned. 'Protestant, I suppose. Why don't you ask her? But not straightaway; that'd be rude. Why are you staring like that?'

'I've never met a Protestant before.' I stood up and went to the window. 'There she is,' I cried. A young woman with ash-blonde hair was crossing the bridge leading to our lane. Leda joined me. 'No, that's my grocer's daughter.' She cocked her head to one side. 'Someone's fumbling at the door. Go and open it, Anna. It must be her. She'll be loaded up.'

'How do you do?' I said, standing before Thea like a hanging *salame*.

'Hello. You must be Anna. Can you give me a hand with these wretched bottles?'

She bent to pick them up and I saw her mass of short, curly brown hair, darker than mine.

'So, you're going to be my official guide,' she said, straightening up and giving me a long hard look.

'I hope so,' I muttered, wishing I could say something witty and original.

'Girls, it's on the table!' From the lounge came the smell of Leda's flaky pastry. I realised I was hungry. So did Thea. We tucked into the panini and praised Leda's cannoli filled with chocolate mousse.

'Nobody takes me as being Australian, you know. They can't place me,' Thea told us while we sipped coffee.

'Everybody takes me for a German,' I remarked.

Thea put her cup down and scrutinised me. 'I wouldn't.'

'But even German tourists ask me for directions in German.'

'Is that right? You look very Italian to me,' she added, glancing at my sandals.

Leda hid her amusement behind a napkin. 'Another *caffe*?' she asked.

'I want to spend the next two days browsing around on my own, just to get a feel for Venice,' Thea said. 'I want to bask in the light and indulge myself with its sounds and smells. I'll do the bridges and churches with you later on. Can you take me to the Basilica and Piazza San Marco on Friday?' she asked. 'I like to do things in depth.'

'Yes, of course,' I muttered, impressed by her fervour. This is what being Protestant must be like, I thought.

Leda left us saying she had to cook dinner. 'I promised your mother to send you home early, Anna. She's such a worrier. Tell her that you're safe here. If you need to stay overnight, you'll have to sleep on the folding bed in Thea's room.'

Back home I found Don Mario, our parish priest, drinking Frascati with my parents. How long was the Protestant young lady going to stay, he wanted to know. 'Here's your opportunity to save a soul. Don't miss it, Anna.' He recalled that when I was thirteen I'd wanted to be a missionary. 'There's no need for you to leave your family. You can do God's work here.' Mother, standing behind him, kept nodding.

I spent the next two days trying to memorise facts and figures about Venice, with Mother's voice droning on in the background. 'Pick up the washing before it rains. Come and give me a hand in the kitchen. It's time to start kneading the pasta and making the tomato sauce.' I hid in the attic. 'Leda shouldn't take advantage of you,' Mother snapped when I reappeared to set the table. 'She should look after her own guests, not have you do it.'

I reminded Mother that Leda's knees were giving her trouble and managed to convince her that I was performing two good deeds, helping an elderly relative and doing my Catholic duty as Don Mario had instructed. 'Besides,' I added, 'this is an opportunity to pick up some idiomatic English. Next year I'll do well in my foreign language class.'

The night before my first outing with Thea I couldn't go to sleep. I was figuring out ways to impress her and gain her trust. I must speak slowly, clearly and look confident. If she asked difficult questions I'd suggest we deal with them later. During the long ride in the train to Leda's place I planned to memorise all the facts I'd learned. Before turning the light off I reminded myself that my primary aim was bringing Thea into the Fold.

At dawn I dozed off and dreamt of Thea facing God on the day of the Last Judgement. God directed her and a group of other Protestants towards Hell. I pushed through the crowd and said that if she was sent there I'd follow her. God looked confused.

I woke up bathed in perspiration and searched for the book the priest had suggested I give Thea. I checked the title, *The Road to Salvation*, then slipped it into my handbag.

At nine sharp I knocked on Leda's door. Thea was ready and we left straight away. She had her own plan and stopped every time we crossed a bridge to take photos from different angles. What was the bridge called? What could I tell her about it?

'Every bridge has a story. More than one in fact. This one is called the Honest Woman's Bridge, and has four stories woven around its name,' I told her.

'Great. Next Monday we'll do nothing but bridges. All of them, if possible.'

'All four hundred and eleven? In one day?'

'As many as we can fit in. Why are you stopping? I can't wait to get there.'

'Where?'

'Piazza San Marco. Don't tell me you've forgotten.'

We were very close. A few more steps and we stood at the far end of the Piazza facing the Basilica which was shimmering in the heat. I heard her gasp. 'It's true,' she blurted out a few minutes later. 'It does look like a painting.'

'Aren't you going to take a photo?'

'I'm taking a mental one, first,' she said, leaning against a column with a rapturous expression. I stood by her side thinking how privileged I was to be rediscovering my city through the eyes of a foreigner and a Protestant one at that. When she finally stirred, she asked, 'Where's the Florian? I'm dying for an iced coffee.'

'At the Florian? You must be joking. It'll cost us an eye of our head.'

'You mean an arm and a leg? Hey, I like that. Say it again.'

'*Un occhio della testa,*' I repeated.

She entered it in her book.

'The Florian's one of the most famous cafés in the world. Don't tell me you haven't been inside. I just have to see those paintings under glass and sink into those velvet chairs.'

'Wait till you see the prices on the menu.'

'All right, you meanie. We'll have a look from the outside today and listen to the music but I'll take you there with Leda before I leave.'

On very hot days Leda insisted we have lunch at her place and take a nap before resuming our explorations. In the penumbra of the cool bedroom, flat on our backs, Thea and I talked about ourselves. I was waiting for the opportunity to broach the subject of religion which was beginning to feel like a burden. I wondered whether Thea had started reading the book I'd placed on her bedside table. At the same time I didn't want to be pushy. It might backfire. Once I've pointed the way to salvation, my duty will be done, I reassured myself. It was up to God to do the rest.

'Most of the notes I'm taking are for my father but some are for me,' Thea said. 'I'm interested in all kinds of fabrics: velvet, damask, raw silk, you name it. I especially like the soprarizzo velvet with its precious stones and metals.' Her words conjured up a world of luxury.

'Does your family want you to work in that area?'

'Want me? Of course not. It's my idea. But first I'm going to finish an honours degree in languages and then travel around. It's my life. I can do what I want with it.'

Her words danced in red letters before my eyes as I looked out the train window on my way home. It's my life. I can do what I want with it. Being Protestant meant freedom. How could I expect Thea to give that up? Did I have the right to try and influence her?

We spent three full days exploring the Bellini exhibition. 'Those gowns are the most sumptuous I've ever seen,' Thea exclaimed. When she wasn't talking she was taking notes. Next to the names of each fabric she entered details of variations in style and texture.

'My favourite colours are indigo, antique gold and the watery tones of the sea,' she told me one evening as we were returning to the flat, pushing through the crowds of tourists.

During one lunch break at the rosticceria, near the Rialto Bridge, she perused the dishes on display as though they were precious objects.

'What's that black concoction?'

'A squid risotto. They leave the ink in for flavour. I'll order it and you can have some.'

She was reluctant but after a sniff and taste she declared that she wanted to try all the rice dishes.

'The smells of Venice are mind-blowing,' she said. 'When we went through that lane this morning I could smell rising damp, brine, pastry, coffee and even the scent of gardenias, all mixed together. Wow, so sensual.' She inhaled, eyes half closed.

I nodded, my mouth full of squid. How could I possibly match her eloquence? I didn't have the freedom to explore different cultures and visit foreign places like she did. She was able to mix with people of any religion without having to convert them. At one stage she'd even mentioned taking a trip to England and Scotland to visit her mother's family. After that she was going to follow the silk routes of Asia all the way to Singapore and then catch a boat back to Australia.

I decided that it was time for me to plunge in and get the conversion business over with. I asked her three questions at once. 'Have you read the book I left on your bedside table? What did you think of it?' and 'Would you like to go to Mass with me next Sunday?'

'Mass? In the Basilica? I'd love to.'

'Are you interested in Catholicism?'

'Yes, in the rituals and the colours. To me your Mass is pure theatre.'

I let my risotto go cold.

'If you're not eating it, I'll have it,' she said. 'I can eat as much as I like. I never put on weight.' She switched plates and ate heartily, savouring every mouthful. Watching her, I wondered what I could tell Don Mario when he asked for my report.

She looked up from her clean plate. 'If you're trying to convert me, forget it. I went to a convent school in Melbourne and lived through six nuns. I haven't got time to read your book. Sorry about that.'

After a week of looking at Renaissance art, Leda suggested we go to the Lido beach instead. 'Have a break. You're taking things too seriously.' She knew the man in charge of the cabins at the Hotel Excelsior. 'He'll let you use a cabin and set up an umbrella for you. You'll get a glimpse of the rich and famous. They're fun to watch.'

Lounging on easy chairs, smothered with suntan oil, we shared stories from our lives. Thea confessed to having two boyfriends, Robert and John. Robert was a childhood sweetheart. They exchanged chaste kisses and held hands. He was the one who wrote every week. John was older. He worked for the stock exchange and took her out to restaurants.

'I bet you're dying to know if John and I have gone all the way.'

Thea lifted her head to check my reaction. I turned mine to hide my blushing and replied with an expression that she'd taught me. 'It's none of my business.'

'*Brava*. Well said. And have you got a steady boyfriend?'

I shook my head.

'Are you seeing anyone?'

'I don't know what you mean.'

She explained with a flourish of gestures.

Oh, to be Protestant and free and have boyfriends, I thought. None of this religious and family duty stuff.

'You're a good student, you know,' Thea remarked the night I stayed at Leda's flat for a proper English lesson. We were going over some idiomatic phrases. 'You're coming along well, you funny girl.'

Funny. A lovely word. One of the first I learned. It meant ridiculous and amusing, but also unconventional, eccentric, quirky, meanings which appealed to me.

She'd called me funny that very afternoon when, in Piazza San Marco, I suddenly forged ahead trying to walk between two strolling Carabinieri in full uniform. Although they had their backs to us, they closed ranks when they heard me coming. 'Don't you ever do that again,' they said, turning and wagging their fingers, speaking to me as to a naughty child.

'What on earth were you trying to do?' Thea asked.

'If you succeed in walking between two Carabinieri, you're in for good luck,' I said.

'You funny girl. What you wanted to prove, though, was something else.'

'What do you mean?' I asked.

'You wanted to break through another kind of barrier. Pity the Carabinieri stopped you.'

I was beginning to understand but didn't know how to reply.

*

On Thea's last night I stayed at Leda's flat again. I told my parents that the three of us would be going to the Florian for gelati and afterwards Thea and I would pop over to the Lido where the film festival was in full swing. They agreed with the proviso that I return to the flat before eleven.

At the Lido we strolled, chatted with some starlets and drank a glass of spumante. We didn't feel like going back early. I rang Leda asking her to tell Mother I was fast asleep if she phoned. 'We're going to catch the last vaporetto to San Marco and walk the rest of the way. Don't worry, Thea's done karate,' I lied.

'I'll wait up until one before calling the police,' Leda joked.

But something unexpected was to occur. The last vaporetto which was to take us to San Marco couldn't dock. I rushed to let Leda know.

'Your mother's frantic,' she said. 'She wants to speak to you. I told her you were asleep.'

'Leave it to me,' I replied and called Mother, wishing her good night with loud yawns. When I turned to give Thea the news, she'd disappeared. I searched the area then settled down to wait. Perhaps she got on the boat, I thought, seeing the vaporetto that couldn't dock suddenly leave full of people. In a state of panic I hired a speedboat to take me to San Marco but she wasn't among the arriving passengers there. I hired another boat to take me back to the Lido, all the way praying, 'Please, God, let her be safe.'

I found Thea standing tall among a few night revellers. Unaware of the time, she was chatting to an English journalist.

I crossed my arms and glared at her.

'What happened to your hair? It's all over the place.' Thea was laughing. I burst into tears.

The journalist, whose name I couldn't catch, went to get me a coffee. We discussed what to do.

'I suppose we'll have to wait for sunrise,' I said. 'Now, you ring Leda. It's your turn.'

'Yes, boss,' Thea replied.

The three of us took refuge in an all-night café. From there I spoke to my mother again at 6 a.m. 'I won't be back till dinnertime. We're off to the fish market and I'm giving Thea a hand with packing. Ciao.' Without waiting for an answer I hung up.

# Dreaming Havana

## Joanna Kujawa

*To Chucho Valdes*

**Room 411**

You wake up feeling radiance. The lack of lack. The lack of usual frustrations and anxieties. The sense that something is missing in your life is gone. You know that nothing is missing.

You are here. In Havana. Hotel Lincoln. Room 411.

You have just gotten here, last night, with a travel bag and the *Lonely Planet* as a guide. You have some Che Guevarian shrines to visit. You are interested in the spirit of Che, you say. In the self-realised man. The man who is always free. Under all circumstances. Always ahead of the wheel of life, of the forces of history.

All night you stay awake. The streets of Havana are leaking through the closed shutters, with music, with never-ending music, with honking of old cars, voices screaming (non-threatening sorts of voices, joyful, satiated with life voices). All night long and in the morning, all around the clock, you can feel the pulsing Cuban rhythms; they get under your skin in an organic, fluid way. They are like a stream of images flowing through your body, like a potent, intense river of sounds. You hear the voices from the nearby apartment, a grandmother calling a child, the child responding in a crying, weeping voice; kitchen utensils and plates clicking. You feel the smell of sweat and genitals in the air entering the room from the street.

I am waiting for you to come back from the early exploration of the city. I want you to have no specific plans. To surrender to me, luxuriously and playfully. With less urgency. With openness. I tempt you with places Hemingway liked so much. The Spanish buildings left by the first conquistadors who had arrived here in the fifteenth century and begun the conquest of the Americas. The cafés hidden in Old Havana where people dance on badly lit streets.

I am waiting for you as a woman in a green dress standing on a tiny, Spanish balcony, overlooking the Malecon. Across the street on the roof of an old building, a dark, young man and a little girl with curly hair are hanging laundry on long ropes. On the street below is a line of old Chevies with their drivers standing outside, smoking cigars.

'Let's take one of the old Chevys and go to Cojimar!' I tease you from the balcony and laugh. From the balcony you look like a gringo commanding an army of polished Chevys from another era.

## Cojimar

In Cojimar, fishermen threw their nets into the sea as if they wanted to catch all life in one instant. The old fishermen are like Hemingway's El Viejo. Their faces mirror the intricate threads of their fishing nets, their bodies are bent and bony, their hair short and their eyes always squinting from the sun, as they slowly walk the empty streets of the village. The salt, the sea, the fish, the turtles, live in them, so catching the fish or a turtle is like a recognition of something already known but never really thought of before. The old boats rest on the sand in the chaos of drying nets. They used to be attended by the fishermen who fixed them while sitting on the sand and smoking cigars to keep their concentration on the job. And Hemingway kept his boat, *El Pilar*, anchored here, only twenty minutes away from Havana.

Cojimar is not sure of its identity. A fishing village

interrupted by the presence of a big Americano who once drank with the fishermen, and went fishing with old Gregorio Fuentes, the El Viejo, the old man and the sea ...

And from the great waters of life, the Americano, big and weird and talking to himself in Spanish when drunk, became famous. So famous that old Gregorio became famous and the whole of Cojimar became famous, and foreign men and women come here just to see him, the old man.

Strange.

The driver is anxious for you to meet Gregorio and enquires about his house from an old man on the street. You get out of the car for a moment and look around. Slowly and inevitably, during the time lapsed between Hemingway's presence here and your arrival, Cojimar transformed itself from a fishing village into the place where Hemingway kept his boat.

The old fisherman on the street points out a small jetty where *El Pilar* used to be anchored. He looks at you with sad curiosity as if he wants to ask you something, what you are really doing here. *El Pilar* is not here anymore, the Americano is not here anymore. Cojimar is still poor, still quiet, only nobody goes into the sea anymore. Something happened since the loud American left. Suddenly the fishermen are absent, ageing in their houses, fragile as they walk the streets of their town and look sadly and questioningly at the foreigners.

'Gregorio? *Muy difícil.*' The fisherman shakes his head but shows the way to the driver.

You go back to the car and drive through a few more empty streets. Gregorio's house is not any different from other fishermen's houses: simple and in need of fresh white paint. When you arrive he is dozing off in his wheelchair in front of the house. His grandson, still by his side as if frozen in time, brings out chairs for you. Gregorio wakes up briefly to look at you with his watery eyes, then looks back at his grandson, then back at you again. Something like a smile crosses his face and he motions to you to pull up your chair and sit close beside him.

You want to ask him something about Hemingway, about the illusion of time and fame, about the 104 years of Gregorio's own life, but in his eyes you only see the fishing nets thrown at the open sea, and Hemingway is a shadow on a boat.

*No words*, you think and smile back at him.

## Castillo de Farnes

You stumble into the Castillo de Farnes by pure chance, looking for a decently priced place for a dinner. It is right near El Floridita, a bar where Hemingway used to drink. You wanted to have a drink there and sit on the stool, at the corner of the bar, where Hemingway usually sat. You have left the bar after one Cuba Libre and stumbled into the restaurant. There, right at the entrance, is a picture on the wall of Fidel, Raul and El Che sitting at a table, with a small explanatory note in Spanish at the bottom.

On the 9th of January 1959, at 4.45 a.m., Fidel Castro, El Che and Fidel's brother, Raul, came to Fidel's old hangout from his student years in law school, the Castillo de Farnes. The restaurant, good enough, with the air of bourgeois polish, is a surprising place for the celebration of the establishment of the Revolutionary Government.

The three men ordered mojitos, the traditional Cuban drink (Havana Club, lime juice, sugar and mint), and lobster tails. Then they had the picture taken with waiters standing behind them. The moods were celebratory. The waiters were dressed in old-fashioned black. Fidel and Raul wore uniforms. There was a hint of exhaustion and satisfaction behind the celebration. Fidel seemed confident and almost overwhelmed by it all, but confident.

And Che? Che sat in a James Dean pose, limp and almost bored.

*What was accomplished was good*, he thought. He had never in his mind said *what I accomplished* but always *what was accomplished* or *what we accomplished* as if he was intuitively aware that he was a vessel in a much bigger river, that he was a tool in the hands of history, of something bigger than himself, anyway.

But as Fidel and Raul celebrated, he was already somewhere else. He was already asking 'What's next?' He was already preparing for his expedition in the Congo or Bolivia. Perhaps not consciously. Perhaps he could not even pinpoint the names, the places, but he was already ahead of his moment, ahead of the celebrating Castro brothers. He was already preparing new revolutions, wherever they were meant to take place.

'It would have been great to be there at that moment,' you say smiling. 'And to take this picture of him, when he is so unguarded, when the pose of his body speaks for him. To show him like that in a casual snapshot.'

Over the dinner you keep talking about the picture. Even then, even after the victory, Che was defiant. The way he sat in his chair, like a bored high school student, too imaginative, too intelligent to bother with his teacher's planned lessons. He defied all societies, all rules, he simply refused to be proper.

Over a lobster and mojitos you decide you must meet his wife. The waiter tells you that she still lives in the city. Aleida March.

Her name sounds English. And you tell me you don't know much about her. They met during the revolution. She was a teacher and an activist and later became a guerilla fighter. Fought by his side, in Santa Clara, when he took it in December 1958.

You should rather meet Zoila Rodriquez, I say coyly. You have never heard of her before. You want to know who she is. And I tell you, in a very soft voice, looking straight into your eyes so you will always remember, that she was a beautiful mulatto woman to whom Che lost his heart. And that being his lover she knew him more intimately than his wife.

Why?

The answer is simple, I smile at you the way one smiles at a naive child, she could tell him off when he deserved it. She did not have to play any social games with him or keep quiet for the sake of the children. She could laugh, argue, make love as she wished and leave him when she had had enough.

Your fork stops in midair. You believe that nobody could dump Che.

Oh, yes, yes, she did, I assure you.

You burst into laughter.

## Calle Neptuno

You ignore my suggestion of finding Zoila. You are determined to meet Aleida, Che's wife. Today. In the National Archives on Calle Compostela you are told by a small, energetic woman, who speaks fast, too-fast Spanish for you, that today Aleida should be at the Havana University. The librarian is both helpful and suspicious and somewhat annoyed that you do not want to look at Che's work in the archives and that you need Aleida.

On the street you take a taxi, a brown-red 1956 Chevy that puts you in high spirits, and you go to the university. There you wait more. To kill the time, you look through the titles of books on Che in the library. Absorbed.

A handful of students sit quietly at long brown wooden tables, books spread in front of them. No noise, only an occasional whisper or a bird chirping outside the window. Another short and fast-speaking librarian says that Aleida has sent the message that she can't see you. Not today. Not any other day either. She does not give private interviews. The little librarian sees your disappointment and adds, 'She encourages Western scholarship about her husband and would like to be helpful in some other way.'

You leave the university without rushing. The whole day is ahead of you. Without an interview with Aleida, the day is an open book. With the help of a map you explore the streets near the university. On one of the houses near the university a sign stands out from pre-revolution times: *Abajo Batista Asasinos*, Down with Batista Assassins.

You take a few pictures and continue walking along Calle Neptuno towards the Capitolio when I whisper to you, in a slow, sensuous Spanish so you can't pretend you don't understand: Think of it. Che could walk the street. Zoila Rodriguez could walk the street. You can imagine them walking here.

Perhaps Zoila Rodriguez never came to Havana. Nobody knows. She was a native of the Vegas de Jibacoa district and was not a woman of great financial means. But had she been in Havana, she would have walked streets like this one. She would have walked Calle Neptuno, in her sensual walk, with her hips moving as gently as Spanish caravellas on the seas of promise. She was a mulatto, with her skin dark and fragrant like coffee beans, with breasts like two ripe fruits, with a body curved like a dark violin that allows only a great master to touch her strings.

Che's men used to say that he knew women were crazy about him but most of the time he had other things in mind and treated women with a great courtesy and detachment. But Zoila had the thing about her that permeated her body with the sweetness ... with the fire ... that made her beauty more appealing than the beauty of other women. Picture this: She was walking along a street like Calle Neptuno, white laundry flying everywhere like very personal ghosts. Old ladies were standing on ornamented balconies with tiny dogs under their arms, watching the street from behind their potted flowers: red, yellow and blue. And below, Zoila Rodriguez was walking, unafraid of it all, unafraid of the gossip that the guerillas were starting an offensive, unafraid of the suspicion of soldiers. She walked the street, her hips like Spanish caravellas ...

Whatever was occupying El Che's mind, whatever tactic of the guerilla warfare, whichever principle of justice, all the preoccupations surrendered to that thing about Zoila Rodriguez. He liked her. Oh, he really liked her.

'What does it have to do with the street?' you ask.

Well, this is not the most beautiful street of Havana. It is poor, it is purely local, it belongs to the other Havana, shunned by tourists, unpolished, unchanged, eternal. Look at it! It is not elegant, far from it. But as you walk Calle Neptuno, you fly with the laundry on the balconies. When you walk the street you can catch the glimpses of the sea beyond the embankments of the Malecon. You suddenly walk and talk like a real Cubano. Life becomes more colourful, more intense. You suddenly remember the steps of salsa without any effort. It is not a beautiful or a famous street, it is not in history books. You said you were looking for the other Che, behind the photographs, hidden from history books or academic papers. That's the other Che.

**Capitolio**

You walk absorbed in yourself and do not see the bookstands in the park, the trees that give you shade, the cobbled streets on which generations before you walked, loved, lived. You do not hear the sweet sounds of cha-cha that pour out from the windows onto the street.

You are still upset because Aleida did not see you. You will never have access to Che's mind, seen from an intimate perspective. You will never write the damned article, the whole damned book you dreamt about. Without Aleida's insight your book will not be different from the long list of other books about Che. What's worse, you will never have the insider's take on Che, you will never truly know him.

How did he do it? Che. How did he manage to become himself? How did he manage to transform himself from another middle-class doctor into a revolutionary of the first class? How did he leave behind the daily temptations, responsibilities and guilt? How …

'I don't belong here,' you say as you walk towards the Capitolio. The building is supposed to be a replica of the Capitol in Washington but it makes you think of Rome and Florence, not America.

Old cars, American cars from the fifties and Eastern European cars from the seventies, honk in the late afternoon, Havana's rush hour, although nobody seems to work in the city except for the illegal sellers of cigars and waiters in cafés.

You sit on the steps of the Capitolio. The long climb of the steps ends just below you. The dome behind your back is floating above the city like the soft curve of a cloud.

'I'm going back home,' you say with premeditation. 'Immediately. I will never write that book. Or any book. I'm going back home and I'm going to live a boring life. In the suburbs. This is what I was meant to be.'

The sun is getting ready to set but the darkness descends on you momentarily, without a warning, like a distorted mirror of the world. The buildings appear in their old and unrenovated ugliness, stripped of their previous charm. The air is suffocating with leaded gasoline. The huge invisible machine is working, working … melding together some terrifying collective of fears and rules fed by the predictability of lesser choices …

No! This is not enough, I whisper above your arm. This machine, this seeing through fears and needs and frustrations, this obeying what one was told to obey. I call for grace, for the other mirror of the world, for the other consciousness, the other way of looking. Without distortions. In innocence.

The light of the setting sun softens into goldish-yellow, into subtle shadows that follow the old cars on the street below, trees, buildings, people, like their invisible selves, secret agents hidden from their eyes but firmly attached to their feet, to their backs …

The buildings sigh in the afternoon breeze, the baroque ornaments, the Moorish designs of their balconies bend softly towards their own shadows, as if to make peace with them.

At the bottom of the steps of the Capitolio, a photographer is setting a couple in an old-fashioned pose: 'Two lovers with pigeons around them, on the steps of the Capitolio.'

And you say hoarsely, almost tenderly, in the softest of all voices, 'OK. I'll try. I'll stay here a little longer. I'll try to see it … without her.'

### Café Paris

You do not say much until it gets dark, until we walk into the Café Paris. Small exchanges are lost in the events of the afternoon. The place is full, the entrance blocked by a big, muscular man, dressed in an elegant black suit. People crowd by the windows to listen to the music, they dance on the street. The Café Paris, a tiny place with great music. Six musicians with an acoustic piano, conga drums, Western drums, a guitar, a saxophone, a singer with the maraca rattles in his hands. A thin, tall saxophone player, in dark glasses, stands at the centre and bends his body forward playing the sweet sounds of Gato Barbieri, playing Chucho Valdes' smooth California, playing soulful Hojas Muertas.

The rum gets thicker with the crowd, Havana Club poured endlessly into glasses, with lime juice, with Coca-Cola; more people; more rum; the small counter is encircled by men and women tapping their feet, moving their hips, cigars between their fingers; the prostitutes come and go. More rum, the rum, warm like saliva, spilled on my breasts and tight blouse by Guillermo, a young Cuban we have just met, who does not leave my side and whispers to me, behind my ear, 'Come with me, elope with me, for one time, just one time, I'll lick you, I'll do anything you want.'

I ignore him, caught up in the music, in the rum, in the pulse of the crowd, the conga drums, the whispers in my head, the sweat, the vague fragrance of cigars; I kiss you, press myself against you in the thick crowd of people, in the waterfall of rum, I press myself with my breasts, with my thighs, close to your thighs.

'Come,' I whisper to you, in a drunken voice, 'Come now, baby, come with me, we have so little time together, come with me now ...'

You grab my hand, pushing our way out of the café. We run towards the sea until the street becomes empty and dark. The music, the rhythm of drums follows us. You push me against a worn-out building, the smell of old plaster, the texture of the porous wall on my back. You can't believe the softness of my skin, the salty air coming from the sea, the dancing couples further down the street, you can't believe your own audacity.

Now!

The music breaks out suddenly. You pull down my skirt and jump away from me.

'Amigo, it's too early to end the night! The party has just started!' Guillermo shouts at you from the darkness, a bottle of rum shiny in his hand, and he laughs encouragingly, lustfully, enviously, when I button up my blouse.

## Museo de la Revolucion

OK, so you think that Museo de la Revolucion is the next step to get closer to anything personal of Che. There is Che's knapsack there, his shaving instruments, the urn in which his body was brought back from Bolivia in 1997, thirty years after his execution by a young soldier of the Bolivian army who wanted to celebrate his twenty-first birthday by killing Che. And the pictures of young Che, as a young man, motorcycling Argentina. The liveliness in his smile, something that a mystic would call 'the fullness of being', so obviously present in him, even a long time before he had become El Che, when he simply was Ernesto Guevara, a medical student.

The Museo is a symbol of Fidel Castro's political sense of humour: it is located in Batista's palace, the man whose regime he overthrew in 1959. On a small plaza in front of the building stands Castro's tank from the revolutionary times, probably the only Castro 'monument' in the city.

The visitors here are mostly South Americans and Italians. They look at the displays attentively, commenting, recalling history lessons. Everything is arranged as it would have been in a medieval shrine for some martyr. The ideology of it does not appeal to you. But the ideology is beside the point. It is the vulnerability of all changes, of all social and private revolutions, that is interesting. They are made by small people like us. The worn-out jackets, the mended socks, the cheap knapsacks, are all a part of it. Maybe you do not need much strength to reach meaning in life, to experience. Maybe strength and bigness have nothing to do with it at all.

History is like that: a few unsuccessful invasions, so insignificant that the big ones, the ones in power, the ones who set the rules for everybody, curl their lips in contempt when someone tells them about it. A few idealistic men in borrowed jackets crossed the sea from Mexico to Cuba on a boat called *Granma* and changed history. The outrageousness of small, insignificant men changed everything, surprised well-established structures, defied outdated systems. This is the only lesson worth learning from history.

What if the story of humanity is a few flashes of imagination and creativity over the immense sea of suburban life: the structures, the restrictions that come with it? The few flashes celebrating Life over security. From the point of view of history the few flashes may be all that counts. The rest is a footnote.

You recognise a photograph of a very handsome young man. A profile. Julio Antonio Mella, the assassinated boyfriend of Tina Modotti. You have already seen the photograph, in some book about Tina Modotti, the modernist photographer who lived in Mexico City in the 1920s, smoked cigars and wore pants. She befriended artists and revolutionaries alike: Frida Kahlo, Diego Rivera, Jean Charlot ... It was years before she went to Russia, lived in Paris and fought in the Spanish Civil War. And this handsome, idealistic Cuban man, who crossed her path and became her lover, was shot on the street of Mexico City because he was a young, idealistic Cuban. Tina was walking with him when the shot was fired and his body fell on the sidewalk, a red puddle of blood around his head ... The police attempt to frame her with the murder nearly ended her career as a photographer. It never ended her passion for life.

> *inspiracion ...*
> *artistica*
> *en una sintesis*
> *existe entre la ...*

Julio Antonio Mella. Only disjointed fragments of an unfinished work, stuck in his typewriter, only the red river next to his body, only the face of her lover contorted with pain on the sidewalk.

Why is it that some dreams chase us? Relentlessly. They never give up. And even when we give up on them, when we find some worthy substitutes, some brilliant rationalisations and we silence them finally, something happens, someone else's unfinished sentence on a manuscript stuck in a type-writer, some street, some outrageousness found in someone's vulnerability, in someone else's unfinished dream, and the beauty of our own suppressed outcast dream is thrown back at us, with a power so intense, so irresistible that all we can do is surrender and follow it, never mind what kind of social crime or madness we have to commit.

You walk across the quiet street to a small park and sit down on one of the benches. It is calm and peaceful here. There is very little grass in parks in Havana and this one is not an exception. They are like the parks in Paris, urban, polite, with tiled paths, not like the parks in Melbourne or Toronto. But the trees are old and tall and you can hear the calling of the birds when the turmoil of history is sound asleep.

**Corner of 23rd and 12th streets**

You want to see the place where the most famous picture of Che was taken, the great picture of Che, the one that college girls wear on their T-shirts in the best years of their lives? It was taken near here in March 1960, at the corner of 12th and 23rd streets. Right here at the corner of the two streets. Alberto Korda, the photographer, caught Che off guard as he was watching others posing for pictures. There were some for-eign guests: Simone de Beauvoir and Jean-Paul Sartre were getting all the attention. They had come to the funeral of the victims of a sabotage that had happened at the harbour. And the icon of the century, the picture of Che in his beret, in his zipped-up jacket, looking thoughtfully into space, was taken by pure chance.

Funny how history happens, you say.

Then you walk into the closest café and order your lunch: some grilled chicken with chips and coffee.

So Simone and Sartre were here, you think. The French

intellectuals, the philosophers, the Eiffel Towers of existen-
tialism. And they met Che here and stood right by him, hmm.
You had not really bothered with them since you turned
twenty, quite a time ago, when you read their books and
wanted to be 'just like them'. You have moved miles away
from them, from that teenage dream of being a man of letters, a man who knows with certainty, a man of clear mind.
You have moved away from the slightly frigid Simone and the
all-knowing Sartre, but you would not have minded being
here at the moment when they stood close to Che and his
jacket casually brushed against the skin on Simone's elbow.
A very irrational moment in Simone's life, that daughter of
Descartes and Voltaire, when the thick skin on her elbow
became as soft as silk, as smooth as the inside of her thighs,
when he touched her ... Was Sartre jealous?

The breeze is lovely and lightens the hot day, the coffee
tastes like the best drink in the world, tipsy on the tongue.
The blue and yellow parrots in cages above the tables polish
their feathers with their beaks, people passing by the patio
are moving their hips sensually ...

What is it that makes it click between two people?

The table across from us is taken by a middle-aged couple.
They are dressed identically, loose khaki short pants, the
same whitish T-shirts with the name of a diving resort printed
on it, and matching sunglasses.

He looks away. She looks down. As if there is nothing to
say. Maybe anything worth saying was said twenty years ago.
Maybe love disappeared with the first mortgage payment.
Maybe the children grew up too fast. Who knows? For them,
the parrots lose colours, the breeze comes at the wrong time
of the day, the sensual presence of the people on the street
is a challenge to sobriety, longevity and boredom.

How was it for Simone and Sartre? For this most intellectual of couples who were free from social conventions?
Together at university, then later having separate apartments
but next door to each other ... He always the first in everything; as a philosophy student, philosopher himself and as a

writer … She always right beside him, just as intelligent, as famous. Equals. Yet they both had other loves in life, meaningful and passionate, despite the perfect intellectual suitability that they had with each other.

They must have longed for another sort of love that rational Simone could not quite explain, I whisper provocatively, my knees touching yours under the table, and you smile with your eyes, pretending not to see me but I know you can feel me in your veins.

## Finca Vigia

Next morning, a regular city bus takes you to Finca Vigia, Hemingway's house. The bus is crowded and cheerful. You sit by the window watching the street as the bus moves further away from Havana proper and closer to the suburbs. The houses have graffiti on them and each bus stop is filled with a new crowd waiting.

An old lady who speaks to you all the time, unaware that you can't understand most of it, keeps explaining to the new passengers who you are and where you are going. From time to time she asks you to get up and give up the seat for a pregnant woman. Many pregnant women. She just pats you on your shoulder energetically, says laughingly, '*Otra*,' and points at the newest pregnant woman on the bus. You get up every time and every time a pregnant woman gets off the bus the old lady orders you to take the seat back. It is like playing musical chairs.

Finally, the old lady, her hair bleached into something very yellow, red lipstick on her smiling lips, pushes you out of the bus.

'Finca Vigia,' she says and you understand. Hemingway's house.

It is hot. In the heat Finca Vigia is like a sailing ship, light and breezy. It seems to float above the green hills with a blurred view of Havana from its back windows. There are windows everywhere, open everywhere, allowing the winds of the sea to enter the house from all sides. Books and bookshelves are always at the extension of Hemingway's hand: in his bedroom by his bed, on the wall above his desk, in the living room, in the guest rooms just above the sleeping heads of his guests; books in his private washroom, neatly arranged on a tiny wooden bookshelf right next to the toilet seat.

In the tower outside the main house, Hemingway could observe stars at night through his telescope, or in the morning he could see the lush greenery invading the house from the sidewalks, from the bushes around, new sprouts growing into the house. And the birds sang and the breeze blew the salty air from Havana Harbour and Cojimar.

Early in the morning, let's say between five and six, Hemingway climbed the tower, stood by his typewriter for around six hours, wrote, read aloud what he had written a day earlier, wrote more, until the heat of the day reminded him that it was time to replenish the well, before it would all be gone: the voices in him, the voices around him, the speaking mouths, the clicking tongues, the parade of faces and souls demanding their birth, in a plot, in a description, and in full grace.

In full grace.

So much responsibility, so many of them crowding the room around his typewriter, demanding perfection, demanding corrections, screaming at the smallest blemishes on the page, on the pages, so many pages every day. And they demand continuity, and they demand order, and they demand to be all perfect …

Ah, just another glass of whisky and soda and he would be done. But no, they pursue him. The old man struggling with … what's he really struggling with? … and the boy, just like Gregorio's little boy … and the sea merciless and open as the eternity around them.

And if the drink won't chase them away, then perhaps another hour of writing will. And if that won't chase them away then he will call the driver and tell him to take him to his boat, to *El Pilar*, to Cojimar, and he will tell Gregorio to be ready, and then finally he will escape, and face the sea and face its immense silence.

You don't like Hemingway. So you tell me. Apparently he stole other people's ideas and he had lost that boxing match in *The Sun Also Rises*. He had lost it but in the book he said he had won it. Sour loser, you say. You walk among the shrubs and greenery on the path to the swimming pool where Ava Gardner swam naked and you don't want to miss the spot. The blue-painted pool, no water in it now. Four tiny graves of Hemingway's dogs are right next to it.

Tina Modotti wrote once that art cannot exist without life and in her case the intensity of her life, her political involvement, made her abandon photography. But Hemingway …

You do not listen as you walk back towards the main gate, among the endless line of buses carrying Western European tourists.

'Tomorrow I'll leave,' you think and I hear your sadness.

## The Prado

It is your last afternoon on the Prado, the pedestrian avenue flanked by trees and puzzled sculptures of lions. But it is not the lions that stand out. They, too, are surprised to find themselves there in the middle of the turning wheel of life. On both sides of the avenue grand staircases climb to the hearts of the buildings, with windows always open, always filled with music, always lit like wide-open eyes: inviting, innocent of any secrets or forbidden sins.

You walk.

Groups of children chase each other. Lovers on the benches cuddle each other, hold each other, fight each other.

Lovers.

You love walking like this in Havana, the free walk of someone whose paths are unpatterned, who does not know tomorrow. The seductive walk of a stranger. If you could see yourself now, you would see yourself smiling, not at me, not at the city, not at anyone or anything specific. You just smile.

And as you smile you feel that you are suddenly pulled away, by some invisible force, from the promenade on the Prado, from the night, from the rhythm of salsa and cha-cha, from the dream of your other Self, the more creative one, the more adventurous one, the one walking with them all, with Che, with Tina, with Zoila, with all that has evaded you all your life, and now when you finally see it, hold it close to you, it is already gone, lost, and unbearable in its promise.

# The Bird in the Egg

## *Steve Holden*

It all comes, he knows, all ends, but not his girls, not this, to be told by the police to wait and *We'll check this out first, Mr Williams*. Not like this. Better otherwise, he always thinks, the frail thought helpless in the face of the truth that, all uncalled for and unwelcome, sits sickening within him, a sequence recalled each time the same, each moment passing where another story could have been. Four o'clock and the waiting with the girls not home and no message from Jane on the machine, the anxious ring-around: school, Josie's best friend, Emma's day care; the phone call to the police at 7.30, finally, and the flow-chart logic of the officer's questions, then into the night and the police routine, flat and tired, till Jane's car's found, out along the forestry road, unlocked and no sign of struggle. Each moment clicking into the next, falling dominoes, memories chained until they stop, and stop, he thinks, stop, stop. And indeed a stop does come. Each time. It all comes to an end. He knows this, knew it in the moment of discovery, the empty house.

*We'll check this out, Mr Williams*. The quietness, the black light of the pine plantation, the waiting with an officer, a girl merely, the police radio cracking quietly from one message to the next, the static furze as each voice lapses, his breath pale in the car lights, the thin blonde girl in the uniform holding her folded arms tight against the cold. And his children, he thinks, his daughters, his wife, cold against this cold, hoping against hope they feel it. And cold is all he feels now, the frigid emptiness and him within it, grown to encompass it merely and nothing else, a cold beyond all place and all time and all knowing and dread the only thing to grow there.

At its heart is the dread of the faces of the two officers who walk back to him, talking quietly, earnestly, not meeting his eye, there on the forest track, and *I'm afraid we believe we've found them, Mr Williams. It's very bad.* Said quickly, evenly, and no way to say things otherwise. But three of them went in, so one remains, he thinks, so one remains, and why? Hope there, he recalls, or the echo of hope, almost familiar.

*What is it?* He hears his voice, surprised, the voice tight and strained to his ears: his voice certainly, but distant somehow and only his lips moving and what to do with his hands? *What do you mean?* Words requiring all his concentration. The older one has a hold of his elbow now, a gesture of protection, solace, consolation, and he knows the truth the man would wish not to tell, known as though he always knew it.

The woman fits the description he's given, and the little girl. A blue coat, he'd said. The younger girl? A blue coat. Beaten to death, both of them, beaten and the necks broken, but *We've got an officer with your older daughter and an ambulance on its way.* This is how it is in the stirring of the wind in the dark forest, dimly there, almost not there at all, a quivering in the air merely.

Each moment leads to this, each time remembered, this moment, this way and not otherwise. He sits there, stunned each time with the remembering, falling dominoes and the click of the polished bone.

There's a sequence to things, phases known well to those who've come to grief: the shock first; the rage of denial; the gradual understanding of causes, perhaps, and effects; and acceptance, they say. None of them clean and simple, none pure. The trouble with killings, they say, is the waiting, for closure, as they call it, sooner or later or never. The term brings a surgeon's cool precision to the mess, the pretence that a wound, neat-stitched, will heal. But the police need to open the wound first, to explore the possibilities, suspects, to rule things out. Him first, his friends, acquaintances, Josie's teacher. Anything unusual about Jane's behaviour, any quietness, talkativeness, unaccounted absences, phone calls, unusual displays of affection? And nothing, there was nothing, it was just the way it had always been and now it's not. And the ICU is where he keeps his mind anyway, a shadow ghost to the side of Josie's bed and if she's gone, he's gone too. But she sticks through it – the days and the week and the week after that, her skull drilled for the pressure on her swollen brain, the blood clots to be removed, her torn face wrapped and prepped ready for the skin grafts, should she live, and the sheer urge of a body for life, to live, to keep living, is what remains, what he clings to, since they never find the killer, despite the most exhaustive forensic scraping and one of the largest ever doorknocks in the region.

Closure, he thinks, each day an ending. Or beginning, he reminds himself: half empty; half full. Closure when Josie first comes home; when the inquest's over; when they go to the Children's for the last skin graft; when they move to the new place; when she goes to her new school. The police psychologist has done all the questioning, the boy-doll and girl-doll and the role-play. They've trawled the albums of photo suspects, Josie studying the faces, one by one, concentrating, her top teeth pressing her lower lip.

Life in a new town and he packs her lunchbox now, the careful Rubik's cube of special things, drives her to the school gate as close to 9.00 as it's possible, watches her walking in the yard – this a new thing, he doesn't walk her to the classroom anymore, a breakthrough.

A quiet girl she is, Josie, happy when she's reading and even quiet friends she likes. He has them sleep over, dreads the day she demands to sleep over some other place and him not there. No birthday parties they have, and Christmas they spend together.

She collects bird nests, skinks, stray cats, the house a refuge – he understands this, accepts the need. A place of safety. But the nights remain a trouble, for her, for both of them. The nightmares. Even the falling dusk, some association she has, keeps her indoors. She hasn't told him what she remembers, if she remembers, and if he wants to know he's not sure.

In his recurring dream he's heading down the long dirt road, pine trees to both sides, black shadows, and the path opening out to the logging area where the roots twist and deform. His feet slip and stick in the broken earth till he reaches the flat stone at the centre. He feels sick, pale, sweaty, the kitchen knife small, harmless in his hand, the moon hanging, a skin-white disc in the black, then Jane calling and the girls' screams. He punctures his skin, the knife sliding in, an easy cut, waiting for the pain, but the ribcage is more difficult, requires some pressure. He leans against the blade and, see, in the space, the heart beating, slicked with blood? *Here*, he's screaming, *take it* and

*Daddy. Daddy.* Josie calling, standing at the bedroom door, pale-faced and small in the moon-dim light.

He makes space in the bed for her, turns the pillow where the tears have wet. She sleeps the rest of the night curled there with him, her head tucked in the space beneath his chin.

Bird nests, she gathers, a pregnant mouse, and silkworms beneath the bed.

Yet each man he sees could be the killer, he thinks, everywhere he goes. Men in groups, men laughing, men standing outside shops. He's learned to stop looking at them, to resist looking into their eyes. As if he could discern things that way. As if whatever had broken things could be named, or seized, or broken in turn. As if by searching he could have drawn this random thing to shape. And if he could find the man, anyway, what then?

Late spring and the warming days take them tadpoling at the creek. He watches her wading, nine years old now, Josie, more than a year gone, his child. She wades the creek-bed surefooted and without fear of the broken glass he says could be lurking. Her skin is mottled in the shade cast through the willows suckered along the banks. *And yabbies*, he calls to her. *Might nip you.*

*Best way to catch them*, she says. But the dread sleeps there, deep in the bone in him, and him hollowed somehow, watching this frail child shadowed in the dark pool, the dread cold in him, the something somewhere missing, and what it is he can't for sure say or hold still long enough to recognise absent, the hollowness filling him like some parasite grown, biggering with his own emptiness. They walk home slow, she studying the tadpoles in the jar in the late set of the sun. *Look*, she says, *this one has legs beginning.*

Autumn, and there's a chill sharp enough for a fire most nights. He splits wood with a vengeance, lost in the rhythm of the swing and fall and the cleaving of the wood. *Like a skull* – Josie watching, the tortoiseshell cat in her arms – *easy to break*. She looks tearless in his eyes.

He stands in the backyard some nights in the clear star fell after she's properly asleep, stood in the dewfall listening for the sound of the stars, the shape and meaning of that distant calling, and his senses, he knows, are not adequate to that task. His daughter sleeping and him stood there in the night dewfalling and the sharp air to discern the turning of things and the purpose and how one thing leads to another. He waits like an offering, very still, this puzzlement burned deep within him, urgent and hard, and the stars burn silently back. Midnight and the stillness only, his heart the one thing he hears, the what he knows and might have known caught there in the stillness, each night.

They never go to the cemetery – a five-hour drive now, on account of the move north. No flowers, no tending, no pulling out weeds. Only once they went back, after the funeral, alone, Josie and him – the one big grave and the one little one. For who can stop and wait for death, he thought, or see the point and pointlessness in things? He felt his face crumbled, the pit of the stomach, Josie's hand in his. *Like seeds*, she said. The earth was still wet where the wreaths had been cleared. The noise of a bobcat working another hole. Her warm hand. A child only, standing gravely, her right arm in a cast and sling, her head shaved and dressed. And who could see the rock, flint-hardened, softly worn by water flowing, or see the bird in the egg?

# Among My Souvenirs

## Rae Luckie

> The souvenir seeks distance (the exotic in time and space) but it does so in order to transform and collapse distance into proximity to, or approximation with, the self. The souvenir therefore contracts the world in order to expand the personal.
>
> —Susan Stewart, *On Longing*

When you come I want you to feel as if you've been here before. Make sure you put the handbrake on. Walk the path of grey Bombo granite as it curves through the front garden. The 280 tons of terraced walls are my TAFE redundancy. We had to rebuild the garden from scratch, but we saved the magnolia. We planted mostly natives, to make a haven for birds and butterflies. I keep a copy of *What Bird Is That?* in the sunroom to check out each new arrival. Willie wagtail, rosella, parrot, honeyeater, pardalote, cuckoo shrike, bowerbird, butcherbird, magpie and pee-wee. I try to discourage mynahs, starlings, crows, cats and whitetail spiders. I take a torch on hot summer nights to watch the Orb weavers. The female heavy and centred, the male, slim and light, hovers on the outskirts of her perfect web.

Mind the steps. Don't be frightened if you hear a scuttle near the Robyn Gordon grevillea – it's the copper skinks or the blue-tongue lizard.

The front porch has terracotta tiles and primrose railings to soften the common red-brick walls. We matched them exactly when we extended the house – renovators' special. The kids gave me the rock-filled blue-glazed fountain for my sixtieth. The pot plants are all grown from cuttings – remembrance of places past.

We've lived here seven years.

The doorbell has a repertoire of twelve songs that drives Harold nuts. He keeps threatening to disconnect it. Still living in the seventies, the high-ceilinged foyer has stained grey and white flocked wallpaper and a chandelier lit with electric candles. The dangling crystals need a clean, but you're more likely to notice the pottery samurai warrior opposite the door, or the framed, signed Pro Hart print. It's a reminder of our kids at Broken Hill.

Narelle has lived there since she and Gregory married in 1991. Our son, David, moved there two years ago. Samantha our eldest lives in Penrith, alone. You might notice our hand-tinted wedding photo (1961, the year Ken met Barbie). If you need to go, the toilet is down those stairs, along the hallway and to your left, past the framed posters for Geoff Harvey's exhibition at the Robin Gibson Gallery and Reg Livermore's *Wish You Were Here* at the Clarendon in the Blue Mountains.

I always make sure the three bedrooms are behind closed doors. Ours is always such a mess. I hardly ever bother making the bed. The second bedroom has four or five baskets of ironing and the other is where I sprawl with books and the laptop on our old queen bed. I keep the bathroom we renovated spotless. Kleenex two-ply with shells or dolphins. Guest soap from a distant motel. Mexican oil-burner on the windowsill. Next to it a bowl of potpourri I made from the last roses of summer. Ivory tiles blushed with pink span the walls slashed by feature tiles forming a blue and pink border at the ceiling and a foot below – shades of the bathroom at Mudgee. The diagonal floor tiles are Mediterranean blue. Ivory spa, toilet and basin. Fluffy maroon guest towel on the chrome ring. We use the ensuite off the bedroom. I always wanted one. If you want my advice, avoid two things, ensuites and a television opposite your bed.

I wait in the foyer until you return.

That sepia photo of the little girl in the long white dress haunts me. That's little Joy Mulligan. There were four sisters, Glad the eldest, then Shirley, Joy and Lizzie. Joy will one day become my mother and our second grand-daughter will be named after her.

All the ceilings have that dreadful spray-on coating – the kind you see in country RSL clubs. The only cure for the bubbling and cracking is to replace the gyprock.

I've filled a blue vase with bright salmon-pink geraniums nestled in the soft tips of willow myrtle (*Agonis Flexuosa*). You'll breathe lemon verbena from the oil-burner next to it on the china cabinet. Its back wall is a mirror that doubles the memories.

You cast your eyes along the shelves. A set of wooden dolls from Burma and a soft cuddly one from Hong Kong. A raggedy Anne of Green Gables, an American Indian maiden, a porcelain-faced harlequin from New Orleans. A bell from the Grand Canyon. A miniature jade bear carved by the Inuits. A porous rock from Rotorua – 1985. We didn't steal it. Harold and I were just chatting to the Maori gardener about how breathtaking the geysers were and marvelling at the colours of the mineral residues. He went inside the fence and pulled a chunk from Pohutu's mouth. I tried to say no but he insisted. 'I am the village chief and it is mine to give.' We thought he was joking until we saw him on television the next day preparing to sign the amendment to the *Waitangi Tribunal Act.*

The World War II medals belonged to Harold's father, Albert. The tea set belonged to his wife, Grace. That spike, stamped 1940, is from the Burma–Thai railway. We went to Burma in 1995 with a group of World War II prisoners of war to retrace the missing years of his life. We had that photo taken near an embalmed train guarding a piece of original track that led to nowhere. My cousin Jane gave me the Scottish cup, saucer and plate when her mother Glad died. Like the other sisters, Glad said no funeral. I wasn't game to go against Joy's wishes, but Jane said she was going to have a funeral and that was that. As we sat at the crematorium listening to her tape of the Edinburgh Pipes and Drums playing 'Amazing Grace', I expected the ghosts of the three sisters to come shrieking through the ceiling. The tangerine, midnight blue, yellow and olive coffee cups piped with gold were a wedding present from Minnie and Dennis Pang. Minnie didn't have much English and Joy used to write their letters. The Royal Albert dish belonged to my Grandmother Jones. I didn't know Grandpa Jones was Jewish until he put on a yarmulke when he knew he was dying.

Our house is multi-level. The blue carpet leads you up four stairs to the lounge room. On the left is a happy plant on a low table. Opposite, the fishtail fern and television flank the sideboard. The fishtail is almost too big for the room. I used to have it on the kitchen bench in Springwood. The photos on the television? The middle one is Harold and me with Samantha, Narelle and David, taken in the lounge at Springwood on our silver wedding anniversary.

They surprised us with a horse-drawn carriage and took us to dinner at the Valley Inn on the Great Western Highway. I had lobster mornay and Harold had steak diane. The driver took the photo. He used to work with Harold and ran the business on the side. Later we found out his smiling face regularly bashed his son.

The photo on the right is our grandson Thomas, smelling the poppies in the red earth in their garden. The one on the left is Thomas and his older sister Taylor when they were holidaying with us.

The sideboard is littered with oriental dust catchers next to the etched glass trophy – Queen of Crime 2001. David asked me to take down his wedding photo. The green plastic Ming Dynasty figurines belonged to Joy – we bought the pewter ones in Malaysia when we went to a friend's wedding. Samantha came with us. Some of the buddhas and elephants were Joy's. Narelle brought the cork carving back from China when she chaperoned a group of gymnasts on a training tour. The saki set was sent to us by a Japanese couple we met at Club Med in Noumea in the eighties.

Lizzie gave me the crystal vase when she knew she was going to die. She was eighteen months younger than Joy. I just realised there's nothing to remind me of Shirley. She was the first of the Mulligan sisters to die.

You'll walk under peeling ceilings and between walls covered with paintings and etchings. Some were given to me by lecturers and students at Nepean College of Advanced Education when I was secretary to the Dean of Visual and Performing Arts. They'd hibernated between sheets of cardboard and tissue paper in a green garbage bag for twelve years. I decided to get them all framed when we moved to Kiama in '98. Actually it was 30 December 1997. My birthday. The others were farewell gifts – memories of the towns we've lived. They each have a story to tell.

That's the coastline near Bega, that's bushland near Mudgee, and that's the image of the house where we lived in Balldale. Narelle and Gregory gave us that painting for Christmas last year. Stars twinkling above a green lagoon. The artist painted it at night – near Broken Hill. Yes, that is the Kiama light-house. I suppose it is funny to have a painting when you can catch a glimpse of the real thing through the trees from the sunroom where I teach people to write their life stories.

There are five autumn maple leaves from Maine, dipped in wax and sealed between greaseproof paper, stuck with Sellotape on the sliding door and above them a dreamcatcher dangling on the pelmet. Here we are. The sunroom.

Terracotta-tiled floor – we had that rug made from the left-over blue carpet to make it more cosy. The windows trap the morning sun and the afternoon sea breeze. I had the red-brick walls bagged – the cement laced with yellow ochre. The bark paintings are from Mexico. I haven't sewn for years but I made the curtains. Blue, pink and yellow splashed with black to give it a kind of Mexican/art deco feel.

The fourth wall of red cedar shiplap provides a resting place for Harold's police service medals when he took early retire-ment in 1994. He couldn't wait to get out. The kids gave him the barometer for his sixtieth. The shield? That's mine, first honorary life member of Nepean Alumni. Narelle gave us the photo for Christmas. Her in-laws organised a professional photographer. Family group posed on bales of hay. They have twelve grandchildren – most live close by to them. Our three are 1200 kilometres away. The carved eagle is from Vancouver – a gift from the organisers of the International Auto/ Biography Association conference. I took photos of all the presenters to put them in their textbooks when I got home.

This is where we have breakfast, where Harold reads *The Sydney Morning Herald* and does the crossword. Where we have oysters, prawns, avocado and crusty grain bread for lunch on Sundays. I slice a fresh lemon from the garden and make seafood dressing with a blend of Jalna low-fat yoghurt, Crockershire Sauce (locally made Worcestershire from the Kiama markets) and Dick Smith's tomato sauce. We share a bottle of chardonnay.

There. Make yourself comfortable. Do you need a cushion for your back? I'll just put the coffee on, or would you prefer tea?

# Double Act

## *Kay Readdy*

Walking in as a patron with your wife on your arm. Mandy's idea. She's sick of you rabbiting on about the casino. She wants to see this place for herself.

In the front way so she can be impressed by the acres of marble, the rainbow fountains, the starlight effect. She gazes at the grand staircase, and your pulse picks up speed. What grandiose scheme is she hatching now?

'Don't get too ambitious.' You pull her towards the gaming room. 'I haven't finished the patio yet.'

She laughs. She's in a good mood today.

'Been looking forward to this all week,' she says.

She's all dolled up in her finery. When you did up her neck-lace before, the skin felt soft and cool under your fingers. It reminded you how it could be later if you could get past the pillow-divide.

You give her the biggest smile. She smiles back, and the ache in your neck subsides.

'How about a drink for starters?' You steer her towards the bar. Two glasses of champagne take care of a week's overtime.

You raise your glass to one of the hidden cameras. 'Cheers!' you say. 'Happy Anniversary!'

It's fifteen years since you got hitched. Every one but the last has been a delight.

You stand at the Big Wheel for what seems like hours, but it's only ten minutes.

She wants to play.

'Go on, then! But be quick. I'm starving.'

You'd rather be planting your lips right where the neck-piece sits – there on the little dimple at the base of her throat.

Next she wants to try the Baccarat table. Again you pretend interest, but you know what makes this place tick. There are three floors of service area down below – a rabbit-warren of corridors wide enough to drive a truck through, a warehouse of computer screens as impressive as the poker machines above. Each one, at some time or another, is fronted by con-tractors like yourself punching in keywords, selecting data. All of it necessary to keep the smoke down, the temperature under control, the electric-light bills rolling in. And that's just the part you see. You never get the full tour. Too much secu-rity for that.

Over dinner, she presses your arm. 'I'm glad you brought me here, Bill,' she says. 'It's important for a wife to get the feel of her husband's workplace.'

\* \* \*

Next she wants to go away for 'a proper beach holiday – not that dreadful Mallacoota again'. Why do you get the feeling lately everything's some sort of test?

You're all booked up for a fortnight at Rainbow Bay. She wanted to be right in the heart of Surfers. But you side-stepped that one by playing the breadwinner's tune. ('On my pay?')

You point to the multi-storey complex in the travel brochure. 'Look, darling, we'll be right opposite the beach.'

'Is there a pool?'

You try to keep your cool. What the hell does she want a pool for when the ocean's right across the bloody street?

'Don't know, babe. What does it say?' You hand her the brochure, pick up your packed lunch and peck her on the cheek, all in one, fluid movement. (There are three staff kitchens at the casino, but you prefer her version of ham-on-rye. Saves a mint too.)

'See ya tonight, light of my life.'

'See ya.'

She doesn't laugh or follow you to the door. She hasn't laughed since your anniversary night. But then she never did have much of a sense of humour. Some people don't – fact of life.

But she packs a mean lunch, and always manages a surprise or two. Yesterday it was a baby avocado with the seed removed and a small slice of lemon in the centre, the day before a couple of plastic-wrapped brandy chocolates. When it comes to food, she knows what counts.

Used to be the same with sex. But she hasn't been too free with that lately. Not since the operation – though her doc says there's no medical reason to abstain.

\* \* \*

She's wearing that bloody neckpiece again. Makes her look like her mother. She's all excited too – new clothes, new suitcases. (And you feel like a bloody Christmas tree in this shirt.)

'Nice top – where did you get it?'

'Myers sale,' she says, but she doesn't mention the price. Probably cost an arm and a leg.

You forget about the cost as she nestles up. Her first flight – she deserves the window seat.

After the plane levels out, she squeezes your arm. 'Bill, I've been thinking. This is fun. We could afford to do it more often if I went out to work.'

That's all you bloody need – a wife who rules the roost. But you know what's good for you. You don't contradict her. In fact, you're downright helpful.

'Might need to update your skills.'

\* \* \*

From the apartment window, the Tweed River sparkles. What you wouldn't give for a dinghy and a handline. But she's not biting.

'We didn't come all this way to fish!'

You wouldn't normally let a statement like that go unchallenged, but her tone throws you.

She pulls up the covers. You slide out of bed. With a bit of luck, you might be able to fit in a surf.

It's a bit nippy but you're not alone. The bay is bobbing with bald heads. The owner of one greets you like an old friend.

'Been here long, mate?'

'Day four. What about you?'

'I live here, mate. Jim, Harry and me – we're regulars. Stayin' long?'

Too long, you think, but you don't want to offend the only friendly face you've seen since you left home.

You surf alongside him for a while before returning to the room. It's still only 7.30.

She sits bolt upright as you open the door.

'Where have you been?'

'Had a dip. You should try it.'

'I might have, if you'd asked.'

'Thought you wanted to sleep.'

She looks real sexy sitting there with her nightie off one shoulder.

You growl, and plunge in beside her. Too late, she's swinging her legs out the other side.

'Better get moving. Sea World opens at 10.00, and I want to do some shopping first.'

In the bus, she snuggles up again. Seems she's been doing some thinking.

'You know, Bill, if you'd rather go fishing, I can find my own way back.'

'Of course not. We're a team, aren't we?' And you mean that. When she was in hospital, you felt lost without her softness filling the space beside you. But it's not easy to put stuff like that into words.

* * *

She leaves you by the dolphins, says she's going to the Ladies'. Again!

It's been ten minutes at least. The water babes are strapping on their skis; the speedboat is revving up. She'll miss the best part if she doesn't hurry. There she is by the kiosk – unmistakable, that hat. It's a wide-brimmed thing with a bunch of cherries holding the front down and a filmy sort of scarf floating out the back. (She bought it to go to the races. Said she was sick of waiting for you to take her, so she was going by herself.)

Christ, there's two of them! But the wearer of the second, identical hat is taller, thinner than Mandy.

The hats bob towards the exit.

You'd like to follow them, but something says you're not supposed to see this. An awkward embrace by the gates as the taller one moves to board a bus. Then Mandy's hurtling back to you.

She hands you a drink. 'Sorry to be so long – I had to wait ages in the queue.'

* * *

She's in the bathroom playing with her hair. A newspaper cutting has fallen out of her book: a self-help guide for the middle years. The clipping seems to be about a literary festival. Since when has she been interested in writing? Or horse-racing, for that matter? When you first met, she boasted she'd lived all her life in Melbourne, and never once gone to the Cup. What the hell's going on? She used to be happy enough with the house and the garden and Wednesday afternoon tennis. Maybe the hysterectomy affected her brain.

One of the literary events has a cross against it. Lunch at the Town Hall with David Malouf and others. Who the hell is David Malouf?

She's wearing that hat again. You hate the way it knocks your sunglasses off every time she turns her head.

'Thought I'd better pin it down,' she says. 'I see the wind's getting up.'

You file David Malouf away for later, and brace yourself for the expedition to Movie World.

This time you watch her closely. Every time she goes to the Ladies', which is often, you see the other hat in the vicinity. If you didn't know better, you'd think they were part of the show.

On the way back to the motel, you insist she remove the hat so you can look her in the eye. She mistakes the request for flattery, plants a kiss on your cheek.

'I knew you'd come around, Bill.'

You try not to enjoy the gooey aftermath of her lips as you pull the newspaper clipping from your pocket.

'Who's this David Malouf, anyway?'

She goes quiet for a while.

'You sure you want to know?'

'Only if you want to tell me.'

\* \* \*

Eating expensive fish and chips – the view had better be worth it!

She's still wearing that locket thing. It gives you the shits. She wears it every day – like it's some lucky charm. When you ask where she got it from, she says she picked it up in an op-shop.

'What's inside?'

She answers a different question: 'Actually I prefer Frank to David.'

'Who the hell's Frank? These chips are something – here, try one.'

She doesn't look up.

'I'm trying to talk to you, Bill.'

You spear another couple to go with the one she rejected, and chomp down hard, biting the inside of your mouth.

'I said: "I prefer Frank to David."'

'You did, too. Who's David?'

'Frank Moorhouse, David Malouf – the writers.'
'Yeah? How are the prawns?'
'I thought you wanted to know.'
'Know what?'
'About Frank and David.'
'So I did. Tell me.'
And she does – at length.

There are surfers out on the point. The waves are getting up. The beach is chockers with sunbathers – even a lone fisherman on the rocks …

\* \* \*

She says she's not getting up until you have a proper conversation. You make a grab for her tits, but she turns away.

You'd rather not own your thoughts.

It's too early for the old men, and the tide's still low, but you put on your togs and go down to the beach anyway.

She's dressed and waiting when you return.

She follows you into the bathroom, bursts into tears.

Something says these are crocodile tears, but nonetheless important for that.

'Don't cry, there's nothing to cry about. We're having a marvellous time, aren't we?'

'You don't mean that.'

'Christ, Mandy, what am I supposed to say?'

\* \* \*

At breakfast, the locket is in your face again as you stuff your mouth full of bacon and eggs and tomato and sausage and mushroom and toast (you might as well, you're paying).

She's eating low-fat yoghurt and fruit. She chews the banana more than banana needs to be chewed, has a sip of juice.

A mobile sounds somewhere. She dives into her handbag. Since when does she have a mobile?

'I'm going to the Ladies',' she says, pushing back her chair.

'Just a minute, Mandy, there's something I have to say …'

The waiter is in the way. 'Anything I can get for you, sir?'

By the time you make it back to the room, her things are gone, but you're just in time to see two identical hats bob across the road towards a waiting taxi.

# Class of '73

## *Kathryn Lomer*

She looks at herself in the mirror. The dress itself is beautiful. But it's got nothing to do with her. It sits there on her skin the way a rubber glove might. She's seen other women in dresses like this and they look as if they've been born in them, the way the fabric moulds itself against flesh and clings to hipbones. As if dress and woman are one. This looks like a borrowed dress. Which in a manner of speaking it is. Borrowed from that world of glossy magazines and elegant parties, from shops which make you feel like you need a new hairstyle just to go inside, let alone try anything on.

She'd felt quite brave the day she chose it. It made her feel powerful not to worry about the cost. She had more than enough money. All the same she was pleased the dress was half-price. A designer-label dress, no less. She doubts she's ever had one before. Although, when it comes right down to it, she doesn't understand that phrase. They all have labels, don't they. They've all been designed. Somehow she thinks of it as being a dress which has been along a catwalk.

The thought makes her laugh and she turns from the mirror and sashays the length of the room. Sashays is the word, she thinks. Or something like that. Something which has the whisper of silk in it, the purr of the cat. She lets the unaccustomed high heels cantilever her hips, imagines the complex interweaving arcs made through the air by her hipbones. She stops at the far wall, and puts her hands on her hips, does a full turn and pouts towards the seats where the fashion audience sits admiringly. Then she turns and works even harder on the hip sway as she walks back to the mirror.

Do models feel confident of the way they look from the back? She never has. Her one close friend from years ago always took up a brush as soon as they met and brushed the back of her hair for her. The friend always chided her for not taking enough care, not realising that those few brush-strokes were something desired, consciously sought, the rare touch.

She takes the invitation from where it's tucked in the corner of the mirror frame. *Can you believe it? Thirty years since we graduated from high school!* She can believe it. There is something misty about those school years. Like going to the museum, which she usually does on Sundays, and looking through display glass with a layer of dust over it. It's all there, she knows it's there, but it's cloudy and she can't quite see it. On the other hand, if she closes her eyes, she can smell the canned tomato soup she used to have for lunch from the school canteen, can feel the absurd ungainliness of wearing thick socks over school shoes to save the floors. She can hear the exact pitch of the siren which called them inside. She can feel the flick of a boy's ruler under her skirt, the swift brush of breeze against her thighs. She can remember the faint arousal it brought on, that sudden heat inside her pants. She can feel it now.

An image jumps into her mind of a day on the beach. She went there with Sean McBride. They were an item for a little while after they finished school. They lay side by side on towels on the sand. He slid his hand underneath her and inside her bikini. She lay as still as still. It was as if the sun on her skin were making it happen, which made it all right. It was all she could do not to writhe. She almost managed to control her breathing but soon it changed pace and the woman closest to them on the sand picked up her infant child and hurried away with a deliberate sandy flick of her beach towel. Right there on the sand, Sean McBride gave her an orgasm. Her first. With a boy, anyway. She bit down against crying out and got her breathing back to normal. By her side Sean let out a small moan of his own. The whole time, she was facing the other way.

Oh my god, she thinks. What if he's there?

She'd forgotten all about that scrambly kind of going steady, furtive hands inside things, and nothing much said. Sex became so different later on. So easy. Too easy. Oh well, he probably wouldn't remember that particular episode even if he was there. And besides, it would be kind of interesting to see what he was like now. What any of them were like.

*Join us for a cocktail party at 5 p.m. and take it from there!* That was the word which made her rush out and buy the dress. Cocktail. What a word. Cock-tail! She has never actually been to a cocktail party and knew that nothing she had in her wardrobe would fit the bill. So she walked into the store and said she wanted a cocktail dress. This filmy, swingy dress with its shoestring satin straps is what she chose.

Will she tell them? she wonders. Will she tell them about her job? She could say that in some cultures her position would be esteemed, like that of a shaman or priestess, assisting the dead in their crossing from one world to another. In India, she is sure, she would be honoured for her work. Although – she frowns at herself in the mirror – did they need someone like her for cremations? Probably the preparation was done by family, the way it used to be here. She feels it as a privilege. Being privy to the great mystery of life, something like that.

Anyway, who knows what the others will have done with themselves? There isn't a single one she's stayed in touch with. But then again, there aren't many live ones at all who she is in touch with. In touch. She sometimes wonders if it's the quiet of her work, the way she communes in silence rather than through endless chatter. Yes, she enjoys that.

The talk is what she fears. Small talk. And big talk. Ideas and books and travel. It isn't as if she hasn't travelled. She has.

She's been to India. She's even swum in the Ganges for heaven's sake. She was booked into an ashram further north, but somehow never got there. The thought of all those other people with whom she was meant to strike up a relationship somehow put her off. So she stayed on in the city, drinking tea on the rooftop of her room, listening to the endless din made by so many people. She found she liked the anonymity. She told herself at the time, it was meditative. She was going inside herself. That's what you did in India after all, didn't you. Some things filtered through to her despite her seclusion. Things about the class system that was supposed not to exist anymore. She gleaned such things through overheard conversations, from the woman who came to clean and bring her meals. So what? There were unspoken class distinctions in this society. To do with social standing and education and employment. The day she bought the dress she overheard a well-dressed mother saying to her well-dressed daughter, who was trying to choose a jacket, that she thought the blue one was more classy. Classy. It has class. Funny way to put it.

She laughs as it occurs to her this is a *class* reunion. Class of '73. And she realises that, even at the time, at the age of fifteen, she could have accurately listed all her classmates in a social class hierarchy. The only one she would have had trouble placing was herself. Somewhere below the middle probably but not at the bottom. The one who was at the bottom, well, she doubts she'll be there tonight. And now she herself could be labelled untouchable. Someone who does the dirty work.

Untouchable. The word wounds. The last to touch her was her niece, her sister's daughter. Whenever she visited she would take the skin of her aunt's elbows between thumb and finger and laugh out loud at the way the skin pinched out and only slowly returned to its original shape. In the end this became just too tiresome to stand. They lost touch.

She pinches the skin of her left elbow now. Yes, despite all her lotions and oils, the skin is like a piece of child's play dough left out overnight. It makes her think of the Hansel and

Gretel story she used to read to that niece. As if she can be tested at the elbow to see if she's too tough to pop in the oven. But she is used to moulding skin which has lost its pliancy, gently patting and pushing a face into an expression of serenity or, at the very least, one relieved of the hard lines of pain. As for warm flesh, she wouldn't really know what to do with that in her hand anymore. She has found herself wondering if, after all these years without being touched by a man, or anyone, let alone having sex, she might have returned to a state of virginity. Now that would be a good question for the nuns.

Surely they won't have asked the nuns along. They'd be too old. Or dead. A feeling of panic strikes her. Look at this dress, revealing her neck, chest, shoulders, arms. Its wafty fabric clinging to her shape. Her shape a little too curvaceous. She wouldn't call it fat. But fleshy, yes. No nun could approve of that. Flesh was a word they weren't keen on. But no, not one of those girls would have invited a nun. She's certain of it. All the same, the dress might not be the thing. After all it is a cocktail party in this town. It isn't Sydney or London. People will probably drink beer and wear jeans.

She worries now, thinking how terrible to be the only one dressed to the nines. Dressed to kill. That would be very uncomfortable. She doesn't want to stand out. That's why she bought the dress in the first place, to blend in by having an outfit appropriate to the occasion. She was hasty. It was the word which bamboozled her. Cock. Tail. Tall clinky glasses full of drinks in exotic colours, decorated with pieces of fruit and fancy swizzle sticks.

She catches sight of the clock on the wall. My god. Quarter to five. She needs to make up her mind. She pulls off the dress and rummages in a drawer for a shirt with three-quarter sleeves. Those elbows won't embarrass her. She grabs a pair of jeans, not her old blue jeans, but a dressy black pair. Dressy, yes, but she couldn't call them classy. Not in a million years. She looks at herself critically in the mirror. Now she looks plain fat instead of fleshy, rolls of black cotton gathering at her thighs.

The uncomfortable feeling in her stomach takes her right back to high school. The night of a school dance. The dread about what to wear. Her mother telling her it's not what you wear on the outside but what you're like on the inside which counts. The trouble was she felt even less confident about the inside although she couldn't tell her mother that. She wishes her mother were here now to say something soothing. She conjures up an image of her, the last image, at the chapel viewing. Whoever got her ready did a lovely job. There seemed so much to tell her. These days she talks to her people, and wonders if their loved ones have said the things they wished. In her experience, there was hardly ever time.

Her partner for the first dance that night was chosen by drawing names from a hat. She drew the shortest boy in the class. The shortest straw. His name was Darren. She's distracted by wondering how many people will take partners tonight. Even if they have them, they might not bring them. It wouldn't be much fun. People would end up saying, *You had to be there,* all night. Explaining. She sent back the form with the box ticked for one person.

A few years later, soon after she began her work, Darren came to her. He'd been in a motorcycle accident. She was shocked to see him. If he were able to go tonight, he'd probably be the tallest of them all. Gone from boy to man in a few years. And his body, as she dressed it, so very beautiful. She apologised to him for being ashamed of him the night of the dance. She wishes she could dance with him tonight and make up for it. She wonders if anyone else will be missing like Darren. Really missing. Missing in action.

A quarter to six. Well, she doesn't want to be the first one there. What if no one recognised her when they came in? Better to slip in among everyone quietly. Perhaps a skirt that doesn't show those thighs.

The ring of the phone makes her jump. She looks at herself in the mirror and lets the machine answer. Music and a hubbub of talk in the background. Someone shrieks with laughter. *Pen!* a voice says. *Where are you, Pen? Did you remember it was at five? Maybe you've lost the invite or something and got mixed up. Anyway we're all here. You wouldn't believe it. It's so weird. Wait till you see everyone!*

Turnip thighs, they used to call her, this woman on the phone and her friend. Then they'd pretend to be nice and say it was just puppy fat and she'd grow out of it. Her voice is exactly the same as thirty years ago.

She walks over to the fridge and takes out an open bottle of wine. Pours herself a drink. Better catch up, she thinks, or I'll be even more out of things. She'd always felt out of things, like she didn't quite fit. Her mother told her it was because she was special, chosen for something else, not just to be one of the crowd. When all she wanted was to be one of the crowd. Thank goodness you get over that stage, she thinks to herself. I'm pretty happy with myself these days. Independent, a job which keeps me in touch with people, even if they are deceased, money, my own house.

She takes a skirt from the closet. It's one she usually wears to work because it's loose and comfortable. She sniffs the fabric. She hardly notices the smell of the disinfectants any-more, except first thing on a Monday morning. But she's seen people step away from her in the line at the supermarket. The skirt seems fine. She pulls off the jeans, puts on the skirt. Better. She pours another glass of wine, one eye on the clock. Twenty-five past six. That's OK. It will only take fifteen min-utes to drive there.

The phone shrills again. The answering machine whirrs and beeps. *Pen! It's the new place down by the water, round the front in the cocktail lounge. Did I say that before? Everyone's dressed up for the occasion. Can't wait to see if you still look the same.*

The background noise has increased in pitch and volume. How can they have so much to talk about? They never used to talk to each other so much at school, just stayed in their little impenetrable groups. *A penny for your thoughts, Penny,* they'd sing out as they walked past where she sat eating lunch by her-self. *Not worth it!* someone else would say. She didn't know what it was it took to be part of these groups but, whatever it was, she never had it. She left that school and never looked back. One on one and naked was the way she fitted best. She soon learned that. She belonged when someone was inside her. There were a lot of lovers. And then – she can't pinpoint exactly when – it all stopped. They didn't notice her anymore, they didn't take her home. Perhaps that was the disinfectants too. She gradually came to accept being alone. It was good. It was an absence of feeling left out. It was impenetrable.

Under the invitation is a streaky photocopy of a photograph of the class of '73. She picks it up and looks, not for the woman on the phone, but for Darren. He's easy to spot, still in that final year the shortest by far. Now he would be head and shoulders above any of them. She kisses her finger and places it gently on his face. She knows for certain he wouldn't have gone tonight.

She takes off the skirt and blouse, lifts the cocktail dress up and smells it. She pulls it on over her head. *May I have the first dance, Darren?* she says into the mirror, and twirls away across the room, glass in hand, stopping only to bend down and unplug the phone.

# end sex

## *Rose Michael*

Alice turns her key stealthily, like they're breaking into some-one else's life. She pulls Drew after her, kicking the door shut behind them. Relieved to see her flat still looks the same. Home sweet home: all exposed pipes and rising damp, metal entrails and the hole in the wall. Renovation? More like devastation. She turns on the fan: what wouldn't she give for a cool change? She wouldn't give him, Alice smiles, pushing Drew towards the bed he's thought about so often. She wouldn't give tonight. Still, she figures, she's about done with the city. Or it's about done with her. She's begun to crave a big house on an endless beach with a fine sugar daddy to ice every cake she has her eye on. She wonders if this one wants the job.

Alice slips off her shoes and kicks them aside. She lifts her arms over her head and peels off her top before heading towards the fridge and the gin in the freezer: thick as syrup, sticky as lust. She can already hear the ice cracking like the floorboards above or her futon yielding beneath their weight.

She doesn't even know where he's really from, she chides herself. 'On the rebound, I guess,' he's said. She doesn't even care. All that matters is the present moment: them, here. Now.

She pours G&Ts strong enough to wake them both up, or send them to sleep. She's not planning on needing a refill.

She wants a drink big enough, long enough, deep enough for her to tumble into – down, down, down. Watching the lemon cloud the liquid, she licks its sharpness from between her fingers and takes the few steps to where Drew sits, tentative, on the edge of the bed.

She stands above him, a glass in each hand. She takes a mouthful from the left, one from the right and leans forward to kiss him. He loses himself in the booze on her breath and her pungent citrus lips. With the taste still on his tongue he bends his head to take her bellybutton in his mouth and probe its untold depths. Something hungry and wanton snakes between them. When she pulls away he tilts his head to look up at her and his wide smile threatens to undo her. He takes the glasses from her hands and puts them on the floor, then pulls her onto him so she straddles his lean hips. She bites her lip, knowing she'd usually be shy but feeling different somehow; not quite herself – or more fully herself than ever before. He pulls her harder against him so she feels the fit of their bodies as though no one else has ever felt it before.

Shedding, unbuckling, pushing clothes aside so shoes fall to the floor and fabric tears, they grope blindly towards the centre of the bed. She straddles him again and he's reminded of Lucy, but this is different. This one isn't trying to wrest her pleasure from him, she's not fighting him for it. He runs his hands down the curve of her small white back where it rises from his body like some fantastic animal: they are a two-headed monster, the beast with two of almost everything. They close their eyes, faces turning away from each other as vision gives way to other senses. Sweat beads their skin like salty dew, slides into their eyes and half-opened mouths. The smell of her fills the room and Drew is rocked by it – that is the taste the wet seashell of her navel promises.

She curves forward, licking his left nipple with her gin-puckered tongue. He lifts his hips and she gasps, stretching back up, one hand gripping his hairless chest so her nails dig perfect half-moons into his flesh. He watches her face until his pleasure overtakes him. She rides her own rhythm, feeling him hard at the very centre of her: something to hold on to.

It's as though she's there and not there: aware of that centre, aware of her edges dissolving. She is a geisha with robes flung out around her lover, her painted face expressionless. (Alice's toes clench.) And the man she rides is a labourer, thrown beneath a haystack by a country girl who piles her skirts around him and guides his hand. (Alice bites her swollen lip.) She is a black woman – skinny and lithe as a snake, writhing on the even darker man who has transfixed her. (Alice makes a sound.) He is a priest, his face turned away from the witch who uses him in spite of himself until his features are contorted by her charms and spells.

Alice, Eve, Lilith, Lucy's stand-in – he's told her about Lucy, his former, her forerunner – Drew's lover, Alice … she has no idea where she ends and the world begins.

'Precious,' she whispers, as his heart pounds through the thin skin of his chest into the palm of her hand.

'Little one,' she closes her eyes, turning them inwards to where the walls of her womb suck together, pulling him deeper and deeper in. Following her blood deeper into her matter until all around her is the pressing of cells, the crowding of DNA. 'Come on,' she thinks, gripping and clenching, her orgasm forgotten but still building. 'Come to me.'

'My child, my daughter, my playmate, my darling,' she whispers to the secret not yet begun.

Searching for the right words to persuade the child to stay, Alice can feel the future hanging in the balance. Time slows, freezing somewhere between the beat of his heart and the grind of her hips. She feels as though she's summoning the past and not the future. The small blonde girl she's looking for could be her, her sister, or mother … She didn't know it would end like this: her, here, beginning life anew with a man beneath her. She'd thought about a beach house, but she'd never really thought of the future.

'You're the next of us,' she says to her not-yet-daughter. 'You're the end and the beginning. I don't know what kind

of mother I'll be, but I'll give you everything I am and everything I know. I'll love you forever and ever,' she promises,
'but not too much. I will never love you too much.'

Alice thinks that maybe, just maybe – not despite but
because of all she is, and all she is not – she'll make the perfect parent. She, unmarried, the anomaly, could preserve the
norm. How *Star Trek*: the Borg and her baby, happy ever after.

'How many stars?' she asks and answers herself.

'How far away?'

And then, as if in final answer, she feels the moment when
life begins. The Moment. Like a key turning in a well-oiled
lock, like a door swinging open to reveal a garden in full sunlight, she knows: this is the beginning. This moment. Now.

Alice begins to laugh; she can't help it. As her muscles
spasm laughter bubbles up like champagne gurgling from
the bottle. Drew smiles at the white arch of her throat as she
gives in and takes him with her.

Alice falls, tumbling breathless with only his slow receding
hardness to hang on to. Her eyelids are heavy, as though
she's just had a hit and is still fast in the grip of its pleasure.
She realises she's come as she returns from her strange
adventure: an unplanned dream that stole her from herself,
shook something loose, screwed something down tight. She
breathes deeply, clinging to him fiercely with clenched
thighs and fists. Her face aches from the rictus of orgasm.
Her voice is sore. She looks down at him and smiles wide
enough to embrace the coming night.

Alice rolls off and lies on her back in a pool of sheets.
Around her she can hear the echo of her moans, as though
the room itself is remembering. Hugging her knees to her
chest, she wraps her arms around her slim ankles, clasping
the right wrist with the left hand. Locking herself in so her
tailbones tip towards the ceiling and the still-turning fan.

'I remember when you began,' she imagines telling Ellie
after her daughter is born. 'I remember how at first I wasn't
sure I'd recognise the moment, but I concentrated every cell
in my body on you, sure if I got all the details exactly right

you'd step forth: blonde, female, radiant. My imaginary friend. My gorgeous golem girl.'

I will give her the moment of her creation, thinks Alice. I will give her this: the fan above me forcing out beats of air, the heat rising from the futon as if from a night of fever. The boy by my side reaching out his arm, touching me as if I might be a dream and asking me if everything's OK.

'Sure.' Alice uncurls her limbs and turns to Drew with a secret smile. 'Everything's much better than just OK.'

# Hadrian in Hell

*Delia Falconer*

> He completed the building of the Tiburtina villa in
> wonderful fashion, in such a way that he inscribed the
> most famous names of provinces and places there …
> So that he might omit nothing, he even made a Hades.
> — *Historia Augusta*

I have always been a waterman, like my brother who works
beside me now; at a tender age we learned from our father
how to fill a marble pond or change the direction of a stream.
Over the last three weeks we have walked about the emperor's
grounds, observing the position and flow of the hundred
pools and fountains, noting their distance from the aqueduct,
and pacing out the subsidiary pipelines. Each has its own
peculiar vigour, determined by the share of water directed to
the others, which must not be disturbed by the work that we
will undertake.

It is quiet labour beneath the sprawling buildings of the
villa, discovering the ways of the water and setting traps to
catch and move it. We do not talk to one another as we deter-
mine where we will dig and lay our pipes, where we will place
the spouts and arches. My brother points to the place where
we should make the mouth of the first river and I mark it on
the plan.

We have not seen the emperor but each day he sends messages from some cool place within the villa. The rivers of Hades must have a sluggish motion, he instructs us; the fifth which forms the boundary of Tartarus should be gaseous and boiling. There will be a bronze door at its entrance for which we must allow twelve feet, and crossings at various points across the water. The pool of Lethe must be visibly pure and shallow, yet also mineralised, the emperor writes, for he wishes to fill it with blind carp.

Our journey as far as the capital was trying, our legs unused to such hills for we had never travelled further than our northern village. My tools broke through their bag and cut my back; my brother, who is ten years older, found that his left eye swelled from the thicker air which emanated from the Tiber and was obliged to buy a compress on the Roman outskirts from a woman who sold them by the graves. We did not enter the city, but watched birds wheel and screech in a vast swarm in the pink haze above the rooftops.

At the Porta Maggiore two slaves shouldered our tools and guided us to Tiburtina. Here, for the first time I saw a hill made out of stones, and truly I believed that the goats which clung to the mountain's arid face fed on rocks until I was able to make out tiny bushes amid the rubble. We passed along an avenue of cypresses which breathed plumes of golden dust that made us sneeze, and through a high white wall guarded by a troop of soldiers. There was not one villa behind it but a hundred buildings that we walked by. My brother squinted in the light which reflected from the water and the marble. Even the vast groves of olives dazzled us as if they were made of shining glass.

As we walked along the Great Canal towards our quarters we passed trees cut into letters that spelled out the names of our great battles, and blocks of marble carved with the deeds of the emperor's favourites.

The emperor has called for us to make his Hell because he has heard of my brother's talents.

A great honour for simple men.

It is dark beneath the villa. The cavern is vast and dry and smells like an abandoned swallow's nest. When we first entered my brother sweated and cursed and made me light a lamp in every bracket, but the first sputtered and burned out when I was only halfway round the chamber. In the swimming light we saw deep niches cut into the walls, narrow paths, and stairs which ended at thick doors. We have since traced some of these tracks, marking our way with arrows scrawled in clay upon the stone, and found that they surface steeply in the olive groves or water courts. There are wider tunnels near the entrance filled with tree roots and forgotten blocks of stone; crevices in the roof admit patches of grey light.

Some days the emperor sends down the food left over from his tables, pies filled with swans, an udder stuffed with shellfish. Today there are tiny birds wrapped in vine leaves which we put into our mouths whole, for we are occupied and our hands are clumsy with the dirt.

In the afternoon there is another note. The slave brushes sullenly at his tunic and stamps his dusty feet, waiting for my brother's answer. It should be possible, the emperor writes, to devise a hatch which will catch the mists which gather in autumn in the fields outside, and transport them here to fill the dwelling place of shades.

For a week my brother has been drawing plans for the Chair of Forgetfulness. On the bank of the Lethe the emperor desires a marble couch designed so that when a person sits down upon it the river will rise up and engulf him. My brother excels at such work. His water jokes are famous: the bench which squirts the sitter's legs at the pressure of his buttocks, statues that vomit grapes and perfume. The system of locks and stopcocks is an easy matter, but we cannot proceed until he has determined how it will affect the marble tree trunks further up the river whose branches will be made of spray. Nor can we deprive the thin pipes in Tartarus of the pressure that will make whistles imitate the eerie squeak of bats.

I leave my brother squatting and rubbing at his whiskers, and wander into the wider, tiled passageways which serve the villa. I pass a group of cooks, struggling with a pig which they have tied to a small cart, two masseurs whose shining arms steam, and a room of broken statues. Singing softly, I imagine that my voice drifts up through the ducts and drains into the nests of ostriches, whose great feathers I sometimes find littering the passages; perhaps it will spring weeks later from an egg.

In the dark arch I see the emperor, seated at its far end, in the shadows. I recognise at once the features from our coins – the strong nose and cheeks, the high, mild eyes, the full upper lip above a lower as thin and shiny as a cat's. He stares into the gloom and then, like a statue come to life, he slowly turns towards me. Although he does not wear his armour he seems to move, half-stone, half-flesh, within its weight.

He beckons, and I cannot resist the grave pull of that inclination of the head, the upraised hand which folds itself again into his lap.

Do not be afraid, he says.

He scarcely looks at me, as if to spare me from the concentrated power of his face. He rolls a gold ring over in his fingers which are wondrous, tender things of tiny scars and lines and dark brown skin.

Of all the workers who come here, he says, out of the teams of mosaicists from the swamps who quack like ducks, the quiet ivory carvers, the glass-blowers who chew on the heels of cheese and drain his wine-skins, he likes the watermen best. He asks me how we turn a river. It is hard to describe, I say. Sometimes it is like jerking a horse's head, when it is galloping, at other times it is a gentler art, a simple matter of distracting its attention. He considers this, then asks, what do I like about working with the water? I am struck dumb, I cannot think. Once, I say at last, we were called out to an aqueduct in the middle of our plains, which had already run a hundred miles out of the high mountains to the north. We climbed to its top and the icy muscle of the water ran beneath my hand. I liked that feeling best.

It is only in these glimpses from beneath that I can understand the vastness of the villa: there is a hall where it is always possible to hear the ragged breathing of the sexual act, a tunnel where the pale hanging roots of trees are filled with shrieking insects, a passageway that smells of silk.

One afternoon, in the room of broken statues, I fill my bag until I almost cannot carry it, with marble feet and hands.

When I next see the emperor he is standing on the unfinished jetty in Hades where the ferryman will wait, a slave who will be chosen never again to see the daylight. At my approach, he steps back into his own dry shadow.

He asks me, what do I think the inside of his villa looks like?

I say I hardly dare to contemplate it. He tells me to close my eyes and speak my heart. Sometimes, as I am about to fall asleep, I say, I imagine that I am walking with bare feet across the floor of a large hall, over great flags of polished stone. Each has a different temperature. The calchedonies and lapis lazulis are warmed still by the eastern fires that formed them, while the travertine and lunar marbles are as chilly as a caterpillar's skin. There are girls whose beauty breaks the heart. And sometimes, I say, and blush, I am filled with a sudden knowledge as I walk, of mathematics or of taste.

The emperor is slow to speak, and I think it is possible that he smiles.

When he was a young man, he says, he longed to know everything; but when he reached his thirties he began to fear instead it might be possible. He has wished since that a man could look forward in his life to growing some new sensorium each decade which would capture a fresh range of sensations. Lately it has occurred to him that taking a draft from Lethe might not be such a torment for the old who have desired too many things.

I do not see the emperor for a long time, although I can sometimes feel, when I am concreting the drainage channels or helping my brother sculpt the shades, that he is watching us. Or, as I walk among the cats which live solely on the steam which drifts down from the kitchens, I see in the grave sheen of their eyes that he has passed.

We receive another note. He has asked the consul in Ephesus to send a dozen crocodiles, which might be tamed like the eels he has seen in the northern marches, to take live chickens from one's hand. Or he will let them free, so that their scaled chests print mosaic patterns in the dusty alleyways beneath the villa. As he walks he will be aware of them, always lurking, like the fates.

At dusk I lay down on the high lawns above the olive grove, where it is possible to see the mountains reflected in the tranquil oblong of the lake. The hundred roofs glitter. White smoke from the kitchens crawls sluggishly across the grounds to meet the hot steam from the springs.

The emperor is seated on a stone bench further up the slope.

He says he dreamed of Africa this morning.

In that place, he says, the land was so hot it vaporised their thoughts. Over the long months of the campaign some of his men forgot that they could read; others searched with their tongues for words that slipped their minds for hours, or came out only with the word for water. Even he had found, towards the end, that he began to be haunted by the idea that the shimmering expanse of desert was a third presence which posed itself between every word and object.

I am filled with the urge to stand among the orchards where I can smell the hot waxy skin of lemons.

The emperor settles in the darkness like a night bird.

When I am just about to turn to see if he has left, he speaks.

Yet there were rivers, he says. And mountains. In each of these the natives knew their own deities, which they had seen flee like monkeys, their faces drawn and bitter, their sacred objects clutched against their chests, before the shadows of the mighty Roman gods.

My brother has located two new springs beneath the meadows, made up of sluggish female waters, with which to fill the lesser rivers. Only the Styx and Tartarus will draw upon the villa's aqueduct.

The emperor arrives with his aides but asks no questions. The men move quietly behind my brother as he unrolls his plans across the shades' banquet table, weighing down its corners with the stone fruits.

In the unfinished Elysian fields the emperor stops, and asks the gardener to enquire about night-blooming plants.

On the day that we are to fill Tartarus I wander further than I have ever gone. My brother says to stop breathing on his neck and so I leave him to himself. All night he has tossed in his sleep and I know that he has experienced, as my father did before the completion of a project, those water dreams where he seems to feel the currents coursing through his own limbs, and knows that he must still them in his heart and breath during the night or they will not recognise him as their master in the morning.

The emperor stands before a wall of masks.

There is shelf upon shelf of white plaster faces, with the emperor's same sheeny bottom lip. It is his ancestor room, he says. He takes one mask up, a beardless boy's face with thick arched brows, so that it seems to hover eerily above his wide neck; its lips are so full and the cleft chin so implacable that I feel it judges me. It seems to have made the emperor's gleaming eyes its own.

Do I know who this is? he asks me.

I cannot pretend that I have not heard of the emperor's dead lover, who drowned himself in Egypt, of whom there are a dozen gleaming statues around the grand canal alone, poised as if to step out on a boat.

It is Antinous, I answer.

The Bithynians, he says, were a people who lived on the flesh of bears and the light that gleamed off rocks; they appeared indifferent to his armies as they lay on the glittering terraces of stone like lizards and absorbed their heat. As the Romans raised their columns, they traded flasks of scented oil in the bare marketplace. They observed his troops with as little interest as a cat bestows upon a man. For seven years, with Antinous, he travelled. They stood side by side to accept the mysteries. Yet when the time came Antinous slipped as lightly into the river as if he cleared a set of steps.

He has wondered since, he says, if we do not invent the gods least designed to bring us happiness.

He has thought again about Lethe and imagined that perhaps the draught is not benign, that the soul is exposed each day to new torments.

He pauses for a moment, looks around the room.

I am the emperor of walls, he says, and shrugs.

We have at last released the fifth river. As intended, the waters are turbid near the source, as they race over the shards and stones that we have placed upon the bottom, sleek and treacherous as they pass the fields of mists. The emperor sends his cooks to immerse fifty cages of lobsters into the scalding waters for the banquet by which he will celebrate the meeting of the rivers. They are nervous and complain loudly at the sulphur. They tell us with sour faces that the emperor has ordered them to set aside a cage for us.

In less than a week Hades will be filled with sculptors and gardeners, carpenters and marble-cutters.

We continue to test the pitch and pressure of the waters.

In the pool of Lethe, the carp no longer swim restlessly about the edges, but hang still in the depths towards the middle. They will not feed unless we tap our fingers on the water's surface. Their eyes have begun to grow a skin of white.

I do not meet the emperor again.

Once, passing through the grounds at night, I see him standing on his private island in the lake, his torch held out above the water, as if he expects Antinous to step back out.

Another morning, I find a poem, on a wall, written in his hand, and seem to feel his dry breath still lingering in the air.

> Little soul, little wanderer, little charmer,
> body's guest and companion,
> to what places will you set out for now?
> To darkling, cold and gloomy ones –
> and you won't make your usual jokes.

Our work is finished. At the gates, we are passed by a group of gardeners, squat men from Greece, and others carrying writhing bags. My brother slowly counts our tools as the slaves prepare to lift the sacks upon their backs.

I suggest that perhaps, instead of returning directly home, we continue onward to the south, where I have heard there are lizards with eyes of stone which can pass unharmed through fire. Or to the north, where it is said that the rivers freeze and that marriages are made when winter ends and the men float to new villages on isles of ice.

He does not answer. It has occurred to me that once we reach the capital I might continue to travel on my own for there are many places where it is possible to make a living with the gift for water.

At the beginning of the mountains I turn back to see the villa. It seems, for a moment, through the sunlight, that I glimpse a broken archway, a collapsed arcade which no longer makes its shadow, a fragment of marble flagstone there among

high grass; the emperor's high wall, of rough orange bricks,
the marble long since fallen from its surface.

    I turn my back, I begin the walk to Rome.

Hadrian composed the poem to his soul, quoted above, toward the
end of his life. This translation from A. Birley, *Hadrian, the Restless
Emperor* (Routledge, London, 1997).

# In the Shell

## *Paul Mitchell*

Five afternoons a week Jason puts on his grey pants and shirt, walks down his dirt driveway and drags his steel gate open. He walks across the road and magpies squawk on the powerlines above him, while in the distance trucks groan on the Hume Highway.

He climbs McPherson's front fence and walks a couple of kilometres through two of their paddocks. He keeps an eye out for cow manure in the first and their black bull in the second. When he gets to the end of the second paddock, he climbs another fence and walks across a dirt road. Then he puffs his way up an embankment, through its longer grass, until he reaches the concrete next to the yellow skip. He walks around to the front of the service station and waves through the glass at Tony, who's usually sitting at the console, reading a newspaper. Once Tony knows he's there, Jason heads back to the skip, has a smoke and watches the sun setting like an over-ripe orange. Next to it, Mount Twyford's green is slowly turning black.

Jason throws his cigarette butt onto the concrete. He grinds it senseless under his boot and walks through the Shell's automatic doors.

'How are ya, Tone?'

'Busy as batshit.'

'Look it.'

Tony folds the paper and meets Jason's eyes.

'Do anything today?' he says.

'Part from jerk off …?' Jason offers.

'Not interested.'

'Bullshit.'

Jason looks at Tony. He thinks the fat man should have at least smiled at that comment, he's been a barrel of chuckles for the last few weeks, more than his usual jolly self – you know what they say about fat people. But he just looks down at his paper.

'Shit day?'

Tony looks out the window towards the highway. The top of a truck slides along the grey wall that protects some of Murchville from the noise.

'Got me Mum comin to town next week.'

'Really?'

Jason can't imagine why Tony's telling him this. So he doesn't say anything else.

'Yeah. Her and Dad are comin down.'

Jason looks at the rack of magazines. Kylie Minogue's on one cover, looking over her shoulder at him. He looks up at Tony again, still staring at the highway. It's not as if his parents are strangers to him. But Jason thinks that judging by Tony's droopy face he's really been asked to put a couple of politicians up at his house for a few days …

Jason takes a magazine off the rack and flicks it.

'Buy a few beers … Have a good one …'

He watches Tony lift his huge frame and waddle out from behind the console. Tony grabs two chocolate donuts from underneath a clear plastic lid and throws some coins onto the counter.

'No worries, Tone, I'll ring it up for ya …'

Tony says nothing, doesn't even turn around as he heads through the automatic doors.

'Sad sacks,' Jason whispers, watching Tony walk across the concrete to his white Kingswood station wagon. Behind the console, Jason slides the play-money into his hand and opens the register. He puts it in a special tray for 'purchases'. Smiles to himself and knows they're both good employees – the camera never lies.

He watches Tony's wagon grumble across the spillway and out onto the service road. Though he can't hear it too well through the thick glass he knows it will be grunting as much as it can, heading up the entry lane's incline before veering right onto the Hume Highway.

Jason can't see the wagon anymore, but in a kilometre Tony will turn left and drive three kilometres before slowing down as he comes into the Murchville sixty-zone. Once he's pulled into his driveway, Tony will get out of the Kingswood and drag his thirty-seven years and girth up onto his porch and through the door. He'll have a smoke in the kitchen and leave the butt in a thin silver ashtray. Then he'll go out to his shed and pull a red Adidas bag down from the top of an old cupboard. He'll get back in his wagon and drive to Mount Twyford where, by torchlight, he'll find his normal fishing spot near the river and shoot himself through the head with his pig-hunting rifle.

\*       \*

That night seven cars will pull into the Shell. Three will be late-model Holdens, two will be Ford XR8s and one will be a Toyota Landcruiser. Jason will mark them all down on a piece of paper – he keeps a weekly tally and then on Sunday he awards a prize to the leading car manufacturer. He knows there's no actual prize, but if there were one that company would win it for the week.

He keeps a tally, too, of all the weekly prizes a company wins and at the end of the year he awards a Premiership to the winning car company. Last year Holden won (just), but this year Toyota's out in front of Holden with Ford not too far behind.

Jason used to give Tony the result from the day before. Now he just gives him the weekly winners and his workmate seems to take at least a passing interest in these. After Tony's dad gave up the fruit farm, he took over a Holden dealership, before it collapsed, too, and he and his wife moved to Queensland. Half of Murchville went with them in the mid-'90s, after the highway turned thick and three-laned, moved out of town, and Telstra and all the banks left. Jason tells himself he'd leave, too, if there were somewhere worth going.

Tony's always talking about leaving. Jason comes into work and he's sitting there, flicking through the *Herald-Sun* job pages.

'They're lookin for console ops in Braybrook.'

Jason grabs a meat pie from the warmer and throws some play-money on the counter.

'That'd be fucken ace mate. Same crap job just busier.'

'More chicks in Melbourne.'

Jason looks at Tony's massive gut, the section rising above the console.

'Yeah,' he says, lifting an eyebrow.

'What? Don't you reckon I could pull the chicks in the big smoke?'

'Maybe if you can pump them up.'

It was only a rumour that Tony had a blow-up doll: Jason had never seen it.

Tony flicks through the paper.

'Be all right. Get out of this shithole.'

Jason smiles and swings his arm, motioning Tony out of the console seat and Murchville.

'Go on then. Fuck off.'

'I might,' Tony says and he picks up his blue backpack.

'You won't piss off, Tone.'

'Never know.'

It's tradition in Tony's family for the casket to be open and the body on display. But because of what Tony did the lid's closed on the altar, in the hcarse and right up to the gravesite.

Jason looks around at the crowd outside the church, the people out of the woodwork for Tony's funeral. Cousins in black and dark green suits, an aunty in white jeans smoking a long cigarette. That bloke (Roger?) with blond hair and tatts on his hands who used to work at the Shell. And, fuck, he almost says out loud, there's even Lisa McLaren from school.

Christ, he hasn't seen her since the last day of HSC. She was dressed up as a punk that day, with a short black leather skirt and pink, tight undies, not that Jason was looking. And there she is, the name-in-lights newspaper chick from Melbourne, at Tony Di Risio's funeral.

Lisa teased Tony relentlessly at high school. Now here she is with her hair dyed black (because she's intelligent, Jason supposes), fifth row and listening to the priest's voice echo through the church. When everyone files back onto the church's steps after the service, he wants to go up and ask her what the fuck she's doing here, but he doesn't because she wouldn't remember him.

But she does – at the wake.

'Jason, how are you? I hear you worked with Tony ...'

'... Umm ... sort of ...'

Jason sees a black leather skirt, but she's wearing dark denim jeans.

'At the Shell service station?' Lisa says, twisting her head and smiling like a teacher.

'We don't actually work together ... I come in and he goes ...'

Jason stops himself.

'... he went ... He's ...'

He looks at her in silence.

'Gone now?' she offers, then looks at the red wineglass in her hand.

'Yeah ...' Jason says and feels his face burning up.

She stands and looks at him as if he has a piece of chewing gum stuck under his lip. Jason doesn't ask her what or who she thinks she's looking at, but he does ask her why she's here. Stuff it: stuck-up bitch ...

Lisa looks at him like the chewing gum is blowing a bubble by itself.

'It's the first death from our year …'

She walks through the dark suits, jeans and dresses and sits down on a chair against the lounge room wall. She looks across at Jason then at the talking mob, holding wineglasses and cans. She takes a pad and pen from her black bag and starts writing. She stops, looks around the room, and then starts writing again.

Tony's parents waddle around with silver trays full of salami and olives, nodding their heads and accepting embraces. On the kitchen bench there's a plate of chocolate donuts, untouched. Later, Tony's mother stands in her son's quiet lounge room, next to her always-silent husband, and makes a speech about how much water Tony used to splash out of the bath when he was a little boy. She drags up a small laugh and Jason sees the cousin next to him smile. Then Tony's mum cries and everyone looks at the brown carpet or Tony's pictures of J Lo and Matthew Lloyd on the wall. A woman blows her nose and sniffs behind Jason, but everyone else is quiet, waiting to see if Tony's mum will start talking again. But she bows her head and her husband leads her away to a back bedroom. Somebody turns the stereo up again and Jason lifts his can to his mouth.

The stereo gets louder as the afternoon goes on. Lisa McLaren leaves, waving to Jason from a group of people at the door. He watches her go and tells himself that Tony had to do something pretty special to get a chick like that into his house. Wineglasses are refilled and beer cans are scrunched into green garbage bins. People look at each other and say, I can't believe it, you'd never have picked it, he was always a happy bloke; a bit thick, some whisper, but happy. He'd never hurt anyone, the bloke with the tatts on his hand says and Jason thinks, well, he never did hurt anyone. Then he remembers the sealed-up casket.

Jason goes to sleep that night with his head on a Melbourne Bitter spin and he dreams the Shell is a white, late model Commodore and Tony's driving it, yelling out the window, 'I've won the Premiership' and manoeuvring the building wagon out onto the Hume, pointing it towards Melbourne. Then a flock of sleek Toyotas, flapping their two doors, swoop down and scrape their tyre claws on the sides of his Shell Commodore. Tony's eyes are wide open above his big cheeks and Jason wakes up and shouts, and before long feels his eyes starting to cry. His stomach moves up and down, his eyes keep watering, but he feels like he's listening to someone sobbing in the room next door.

*    *

He gets four weeks' holiday a year and he always spends two of them in shitty Murchville. Jason doesn't realise why until his workmate has shot himself and then he knows it's so he could hang out with Tony.

On days he'd normally be walking across the paddocks to the Shell, Jason gets in his Cortina, picks up a pizza he's phone-ordered then grabs a dozen cans. He drives to Tony's and thinks, every time, Shit, I should have bought more pizza.

The pair sit on brown vinyl chairs Tony's parents gave him, along with the house to rent, when they left for Queensland. They watch pornos until they get bored – or Tony heads to the toilet. Jason waits until he gets home. Some nights they roll a joint and Tony always lets Jason take the last tug. When they smoke they always end up in beanbags in front of music videos, eating corn chips and gabbling to each other.

One night Tony talks about Fiona Beckwith, some girl Jason can't even remember, with whom they were apparently both in primary school. Then Tony says she teased him all the way through Grade Three. And Jason remembers her.

'She was a horror head … And she wasn't the only one …'
He sees Tony looking at him through his red eyes.
'The only horror head?'
'No, ya tool. She wasn't the only one teasing you.'

Jason throws him another bag of corn chips. Tony opens them up.

'Do you think you'll ever get married?'

Jason looks across at the big man in the other beanbag.

'To you? Nope.'

Tony looks at him and grins. Waiting for more deep and mournful, Jason supposes.

'Nah, too fucken expensive.'

Tony doesn't smile. Jason feels his eyes on him.

'Do you think you ever will, Jase?'

He shakes his head: there's no pleasing the boy.

'I spose, if I find the right chick ... Probly.'

'You still seeing Karen from Just Jeans?' Tony asks.

'No ... that's, nah ... that's all over. She wanted to move.'

'To Melbourne?'

Jason keeps watching the video, a band dousing themselves with paint.

'Anywhere,' he tells him. 'She didn't care.'

Guitars thrum and the scene cuts to a girl in black lingerie.

'Don't think I'll ever get married'.

Jason laughs.

'Don't say that, mate. You've got your blow-up doll. Wadda ya call her?'

Tony doesn't say anything more for a while, then he starts talking about Essendon and whether they'll make the finals. Soon he's snoring in his beanbag so Jason turns off the television and leaves.


He walks across McPherson's two paddocks every morning now. By the time Jason reaches the skip his fading black boots are darkened by the dew. If Shell doesn't get a replacement for Tony soon he reckons he might have to buy a special 'work' pair of gumboots. Another twenty bucks gone.

At least they've got Peter what's-his-name to cover the nightshift, he thinks, ringing up a customer's Coke and petrol purchase, so he's not at the Shell all day. There are a couple of busy patches: early in the morning a few trucks come through, then there's the after-school rush. The rest of the time there's a steady trickle of cars and trucks for quick petrol and Mars bars before they race on.

Jason looks out from the console desk, into the growing darkness and the Hume Highway. The top of a truck goes past, a muffled scream from its motor as it powers south to Melbourne.

Where the chicks are.

The rumour's stronger than the blow-up doll. No one's laughing though when they tell each other this one: Tony organised a Filipino bride, but she saw a picture of him and decided not to come. The upshot is, what else could it be, that he couldn't face telling his mum, No, actually, I won't be getting married now.

Jason thinks of Tony – he probably sat here at the counter as he did it – writing letters to a village girl, grinning at his reflection in the window as the day darkened. He was probably making secret trips to Bendigo or somewhere, trying to get a suit to fit. Jason smiles to himself and then gets a tightness in his guts and neck, the same one he gets every time he thinks of Tony. The driveway is empty so he heads out to the skip for a smoke.

The sun's leaving its orange peel everywhere and he looks at the emerging stars, the tip of Mount Twyford pushing up as if it might have something to say to them. All around the base of the mountain there are fires, farmers burning off. One of the blazes is bigger than the others and the smoke is heading right up to the mountain peak and the stars getting brighter every minute.

Back at the console, Jason flicks through the newspaper. For a joke he's been looking at the personals most days. Guy seeks guy, he laughs. Mature woman wants younger man. He looks through the Murchville column and Bendigo. Sometimes even Melbourne.

Girl seeks guy, thirty-plus for fun times.

And maybe kids and a mortgage, Jason says, and closes the

paper. Then he opens it again and takes another look at the Melbourne column. He's still looking and munching a donut when Pete walks in.

'Rung that up, have ya?' Pete says and winks.

Jason gets up from the console seat.

'Stackin it on mate', Pete says, pointing.

Jason looks down at his stomach as he walks down the steps to the shop floor. His gut is barely pushing over his belt: What's this prick on about?

He feels in his pocket for play-money and he's about to pull some out when he takes his hands off them and leaves them inside. Instead, he reaches into his backpack, takes out his wallet and puts goldies on the counter. Peter scrapes them into his hand.

'Movin up in the world, are we?'

Jason doesn't answer and he walks through the automatic doors.

# We Are Not Sluts

*Ellen Rodger*

Tall and thin and hunched over, body shaped by gaps, dips, and hollows, the man's wife looks to him for instructions. Her breasts curve deeply in from the top then swing up to the nipple, and are so tender-looking I almost fear for them. A brutal quality, created by an absence of personalities, pervades the room. Personalities have no place when more than two people are in a room at the massage parlour.

With dry hands I massage the man's wife, not rubbing or kneading, but shaping my fingers to the contours of her body. Her skin feels depleted and crinkled as tissue paper, even though she is young. She appears malnourished. We move and sway, our eyes not engaging, her husband watching with hands on hips, moustache so thick and wide it's a disguise.

The man's wife tips the oil container up, a plastic bottle made for sauce. The oil is cheap, gluggy rather than slick. Hands wet with it, she kneels on the floor and strokes my legs.

Because we are not talking, because of the absence of personalities, a vacuum is created in which memories arise, and in the brightly lit room I'm remembering a day at the beach, and the middle-aged men with elbows poised on bent knees, alert beside prone, tired, bored-looking wives who seemed to not care about anything. I'm fourteen, waiting outside the toilet block for my friend. Mothers emerge, hurrying children away from the frightening sexuality that beachside toilets evoke. Girls get abducted from toilets like these. What would it be like to be abducted? Dreadful of course, dreadful. I wait for my friend, holding my sandals, feet buried in dirty sand.

My friend comes out of the toilet and we walk down to the beach. We sunbake on our stomachs, undoing the bottom string of our bikini tops so that there are no unnecessary interruptions to the smooth brown skin of our backs, but being careful, when we perch up on our elbows to smoke, that our breasts remain concealed.

*We are not sluts.*

This semi-revealed state of my breasts makes me want to be seen, not in the traditional sense, but in some other way, a way I only have a vague notion of, a way that involves horror and fear and doesn't involve my will. I want nothing to do with it, and I want to be singled out. I think I want to be spied on.

My friend and I are beautiful, but speak to each other as though we are ugly.

*We are not vain.*

It's exhausting, not being able to acknowledge our beauty.

There is something righteous about the idea of never attracting the right boys, so I say things like, 'Why is it always revolting old men who perve?'

And though I obligingly admire, along with my friend, the blond boys our own age with surfboards and salt-speckled chests, I'm compelled by the unremitting blasts of flat-out attention from the revolting old men who perve. Mostly I forget about my attraction to them because it makes no sense at all, and then I remember, and remembering is so profound a jolt, it's almost buckling. It's disgusting.

In the afternoon we pack our stuff up and walk to a less crowded part of the beach. My friend wants to sunbake topless, and she doesn't want to be perved at by revolting old men. I'm starting to identify that I'm set profoundly apart from my friend, and am smart enough to know not to mention it.

*I don't want to be perved at by revolting old men either.*

We haul our stuff across hot sand, me listlessly, my friend vigorously, feet sinking up to our ankles, settling in an area where grass is starting to poke through. The serious surfers, not the blond boys we worship, come to this end of the beach. There are no flags, no families, and very few swimmers. The serious surfers take no notice of us.

Invisible against a sun-bleached sky, cigarette smoke loses its sense of nourishment and tastes simply of chemicals. My bikini bottom feels cardboardy from saltwater. How can the texture of an overwashed towel feel better on my nipples than a boy's fingers? Once in the back of a car I got aroused by the pressure of a folded-up blanket which I mistook for my boyfriend's hand. I thought: stillness is the key, he's finally learnt, I've never been this close to coming. Later I realised my boyfriend was asleep.

Smoke-rings wobble and tremble from the click of my jaw. A man and a woman are sitting up in the sand dunes, fully clothed, no towels in sight, the man's arm pulling the woman closer. I try to decipher whether the woman is pulling away, or if I'm imposing that attitude upon her. They're an ordinary-looking couple, perhaps how my boyfriend and I might look in ten years' time.

The man *is* pulling the woman closer than she wants. She looks bored, which I can relate to; how many days and nights have I spent at the beach with boys? Since twelve I've been having romantic encounters in the sand, and though the beach is laden with erotic potential, I have never enacted anything interesting here.

The woman gets up and leaves. I expect an argument, but she walks calmly towards the sand dunes. Where is she going? There's just a barbed wire fence up there. Feeling that I've caused the woman to leave, that I've somehow given the impression that I want the man to be alone, I turn and face the other way.

I don't want anything to distinguish me from my friend.

The man appears before me and asks for matches. I'm so

focused, I can see the rings in the paper of his cigarette. The match strikes crisply. He walks away, then calls back to me. I turn and get the most shocking erotic charge I've ever felt. I could vomit, that's how sickeningly aroused I am. The man smiles, touching his penis. Come spurts out.

My friend and I are laughing, revolted. There is no sense of danger in what has happened, at least not while I pretend to be revolted. The man walks towards the sand dunes, away from us, towards the other woman. A clump of sand hardens and lifts into the shape of a flying saucer.

*

In the warm room the woman climbs on top of her husband. I want to warn her that baby oil will give her thrush, but she has already lowered herself down. Her hunched back with its protruding cage of ribs looks prehistoric. I sit in the cane chair, looking down at the couple's pile of messy clothes on the floor.

# Reading Rilke

## *Jena Woodhouse*

She glances at him as he explains the reason for his request, but her mind keeps shying off at a tangent. He seems to have no inkling of the images taking up defensive positions behind her eyes.

'My daughter lives with her mother now in Germany. They have migrated too. But I have always admired the classics of German literature and music. The German philosophers, also, are very dear to me …'

An eight-year-old girl in a different, distant Germany is afraid of what hunger is doing to her. She wishes she could forget what she's been taught. That it's wrong to show weakness. Wrong to steal. German children do not show weakness, because they belong to a superior race.

If she were not a German child, it would not be wrong to go out to the countryside, to enter other people's fields, where there might be some nuts lying under the walnut trees, something to stop the gnawing hunger. She wouldn't let pride stop her from knocking on a farmhouse door, to beg a glass of milk, a crust of bread. If she were an English child, for instance. English children, French children, Russian children could do that sort of thing. This helps to explain why the English, the French, the Russians, are going to lose the war, as the school director reminds her and her classmates daily.

'… just make coffee first,' she hears herself saying, moving blindly towards her small galley for refuge. But there is no wall she can hide behind, just a row of cupboards topped by a bench. She is as exposed as an eight-year-old girl on the streets of Berlin in 1945.

'It's the pronunciation. I have problems with the pronunciation,' he is saying. 'But when I try to learn a new language, I want most of all to hear the poetry composed in that language. That is why I ask you to read Rilke for me. If you don't mind.'

Why should she mind? Why should it be so difficult to read her own language? The war had ended more than fifty years ago. But how had it ended for her, and when? She has heard it said by people who weren't there that not all the soldiers who 'liberated' Berlin were barbarians. Everybody who had been there then knew otherwise, and in case they were in any doubt, the radio kept reminding them. How could one forget such things? … Besides, she had seen them with her own eyes, the armies of the east, looking and sounding like wild beasts – hungry, haggard, angry, unshaven, and terrifying in their foreignness. They were nothing like the German soldiers she had seen parading, with their immaculate uniforms and sense of discipline. That was how civilised people looked! … She has read that the Nazi invaders of Russia behaved worse than beasts, but one of her uncles was with them, and he was no beast …

'So I have chosen three poems from Rilke. If you will let me record you reading them, I can listen and learn from your pronunciation.'

Two hands are not enough to protect you from seeing and

hearing. You have to choose whether to cover your ears or your eyes.

'Which poems have you chosen?' The answer is immaterial, but she must play for time to compose herself.

If she closes her eyes tightly, she can put her hands over her ears, but two small hands cannot shut out the rumble and vibration of tanks, the sound of boots on the cobblestones, the screams of fleeing women and children. (German women and children, who must at all times show their strength. But who now instead show terror, anguish.) She hears the brutes speaking. The voices of beasts of prey. They are as desperately hungry as the old women and children. And they are winning the war.

'We shall drink the coffee, then I will read.'

How many years had it been before the rich smell of coffee returned? Probably, the Americans had brought it. Her parents would drink it as if receiving a sacrament, inhaling the aroma with half-closed eyes, briefly transported to a time when there had been no need for the unnatural silence between them.

'Have you ever been to Germany?'

'No, but I hope I will go one day. To see my daughter, if she remembers me.'

'But why learn German? What is your purpose?'

'In Russia, we believe that culture is carried in language, and that to be educated, you must know other languages and literatures, especially those of Europe: France, Germany, England, Italy … I study these to educate myself, and for the pleasure, yes, the profound pleasure it brings me.'

She knows with certainty that nothing could have induced her to learn Russian. She had simply been caught off guard when asked to do this favour for a friend of a friend. But even now, she would be hard put to find a convincing excuse to refuse.

'So – we should begin.'

They move a little closer under the circle of light cast by the standard lamp, the grey head and the dark-haired, younger one.

'Ah! "Der Panther". Everybody knows "Der Panther".' It is a poem about a caged panther, pacing to and fro behind the bars which impinge on his vision, at the same time as they limit his freedom of movement, his entire life.

Strange, therefore, he thinks, since the poem is so well known, that she should stumble slightly on the second-last line. He should have given her more time to ready herself, but he had assumed she'd need no preparation.

Strange, she thinks, that her eyes should blur the familiar words. For a fleeting moment she felt she had changed places with the panther.

> Wearied by interminable bars,
> his vision comprehends nothing beyond.

But she has a check-up with the optometrist every year. Long ago, in Germany, she was told that her poor eyesight was due to wartime food shortages. Critical vitamin deficiencies, they said, in the developmental phase.

Reading the next poem, 'Die Erblindende' – 'Going Blind' – about a woman losing her vision, her throat seems to open to allow her voice to pass unimpeded. The light glints fleetingly on the thick, owlish lenses she wears, as her involuntary glance flickers over him. His face is suffused with pleasure at having so dear a wish granted. To find a reader for Rilke's words in a country where he knows almost nobody …

His evident pleasure seems to ignite a corresponding spark in her as she reads the lines:

> upon her eyes, made luminous by joy,
> light moved as on the surface of a pool.

His final request is for 'Archaische Torso Apollos'. 'An Archaic Torso of Apollo'. Predictably, she thinks. But reads with unexpected warmth. After the last line has entered the tiny microphone she sits with the open book on her lap, still resonating with the words. Exactly like an instrument as the last note fades into silence, he thinks.

The last words of this poem have become a commonplace: You must change your life. (*Du mußt dein Lebe ändern.*) And yet they had the power to move her when she uttered them just now. Strange.

The moment passes, and she shuts the book, but her face is soft, reflective, luminous.

He stands to leave. She looks him in the eye for the first time. 'I never realised what a pleasure it can be to read the poems aloud. From now on, I will always do so. Thank you for making me see this.'

Her initial reluctance to read the poems aloud to him still puzzles him, but he sees that she is indeed moved. No doubt the poems hold pleasant memories for her, he thinks. He steps lightly into the night, the mini-CD with the live poems nestled in his breast pocket.

# Distance Runner

## *Paddy O'Reilly*

**Transience** §

It is three o'clock on a black, icy spring morning in Tokyo. A group of people cluster around a cherry blossom tree in full flower deep inside a vast, empty park. Rain drizzles down and the spectators hunch their shoulders and bow their heads. I am one of the crowd. We are watching a man dancing among the boughs of the tree. He is being filmed. He has shaved his entire body and covered his skin in white greasepaint. Only his black eyes and the scarlet cavern of his mouth show against the white. The camera films his grimaces and contortions as he wraps his thick, sturdy limbs around the branches of the tree. Each time he moves, the tree lets fall a sprinkle of pink petals and they adorn the hair and shoulders of the audience like confetti. Tom hands me a paper cup with a dribble of hot sake in the bottom and a cherry blossom petal pasted to the outside of the cup. As I raise the cup to my lips and taste the steaming drink I suddenly understand why cherry blossoms are so important. They show how transient life is. They are exquisite for a moment and then they are gone. Every petal will be dead and fallen within a week. And then I shiver because I am cold and hungry and tired, and most of all I am lonely.

---

§  Let's say I told you this story and you asked me, *Is that a dream you had?* I would answer, *No, that is my life on the night of my thirty-third birthday.*

## Enclosure

We step into a room where a different crowd is milling around an auditorium. Without warning all light is extinguished and hands begin to touch us, herding us roughly into what seems to be a line. I can hear the breathing and coughs of bodies around me, but the room is completely without light and even after a few minutes I am still blind. Someone further ahead giggles nervously and is shushed. A hand grips my elbow and pushes me forward until I reach a ladder. I climb the ladder. At the top I crawl on all fours across a platform, sometimes bumping my head into the buttocks or the shoulders of another anxious body. *Sorry*, we whisper to each other. I find a wall and sit against it, feeling the probing hands of other people brush my body and hurriedly pull away as they search for their own safe space. When everything is finally quiet except for the breathing of the crowd, a voice tells us to stand up and once we are all on our feet the box containing us begins to move. There is nothing to hold on to except the walls or other people. We stumble as the box glides around. I hit my head against the wall and I feel tears start in my eyes. Just as the tension has risen to the point where we are ready to rebel, the lights flood on inside the box, a trapdoor in the side wall slides open, and a grotesque puppet head lunges through the hole and screams with laughter. *Scared?* it shouts. Ω

---

Ω  If I told you this you might laugh and say, *Well, you shouldn't keep going to see experimental theatre.* And I would probably answer, *These shows sometimes hint at how your own life is going.* What would you say to that? I imagine you would say, *Oh, you drama queen.*

## Supplication Ψ

We take a trip to Enoshima, home of the goddess of the arts. In midsummer the humidity wraps around us like the cling-ing arms of hot children and even before we have walked the whole way across the bridge to the island I am flagging. We stop in the dusty town square to buy a drink. Outside the fish shop is a fibreglass statue of Benten, the goddess of the arts. Her black hair is pulled back from her face and held with a comb at the back. She wears a kimono draped over one shoul-der so that her right breast shows. On her lap sits a lute. *Take a photo*, I tell Tom. He wants me to stand next to the statue and put my arm around her naked shoulder but I prefer the picture of her alone, staring out across the bridge towards the mainland with a baleful expression as if she is wondering why she has been banished to this faded tourist island.

At the top of the hill there is a shrine where we buy lucky charms because Benten is one of the lucky gods. Tom buys a key ring with a glass vial attached. Inside the vial is a minia-ture statue of Benten. A man next to us at the stall warns us about Benten. *She is a very jealous goddess*, he says. *You must not have other gods near her or she will be jealous of your love for them. She wants you all to herself. If she catches you with someone else she will destroy your artistic powers, take away all your money, ruin your life.*

By the time we are trudging down the hill back to the tram stop, I am exhausted. Tom strides ahead then waits for me to catch up. The afternoon sun bores through my black straw hat, but when I take off the hat the sun's rays burn the skin of my face. I am wearing a short dress with thin straps and my shoulders are turning bright pink. Men turn to stare when I

Ψ Just like everywhere else, the gods in Japan are capricious. The link between what you have done wrong and why you are being punished is rarely clear. Do you remember when you saw my collection of brightly coloured charms and prayers to the different gods? When I told you I was covering all my bets you said, *That only works if you know the whole field.* I laughed at you then. *Does this mean you're afraid?* I asked.

finally sit down on the kerb to rest and try to tug my tight dress further down my thighs. Tom strolls back to where I sit. He stands in front of me, blocking the sun. *Stay there a minute will you?* I say. *It's very cooling.* He lifts his arm to shade his eyes and I see that the Benten key ring is looped around his middle finger. The charm dangles from his hand, and Benten's tiny body rattles around in her glass cage as Tom wipes the sweat from his forehead.

*That's no way to treat a goddess,* I say to him. *Do you mind if we rest in a coffee shop for a while?*

He laughs and takes the key ring off his finger, then places it with mock respect in his pocket. But the image of her dangling from his finger, trapped in her glass prison, has lodged in my mind. We sit in a coffee shop and drink iced tea and wait until I feel ready to set off again.

**Patience** ⍵

This day I am waiting in a dim corridor. People occasionally walk by. One or two nod. I sit there for an hour listening to bodies moving about in the room opposite my seat. Finally I am allowed in. There is an audience of three, all dressed in lead costumes. I am the performer. The three leaden people move behind a screen. Two arms, encased in lead-shielded gloves, reach out from behind the screen and take the lid off a container, then use tongs to pull out a large pill which they place in my hand. I swallow the pill, then wash it down with a glass of water. The leaden people are all standing far away, but one of the people takes off her mask. It is the woman doctor I know well. She smiles at me and tells me I have been good. I remember her with fondness. She is the woman who has said to me over the past few months in her broken English, *Do not be exciting. You can die. Remember, no exciting.*

*It's all right*, I always assured her. *I am not exciting.*

That night I say to Tom, *I can't sleep with you. I have to be alone.*

He pauses. He looks around the room and frowns. *Oh, OK*, he says.

*I mean*, I say, *they told me that I'm dangerous. I'm sending out radiation. I'm not allowed to sleep next to anyone for two nights.*

*Oh. Right. Right, OK, I see*, he says. *So do you need anything?*

---

⍵ When you are sick for a long time, you learn to wait in a new way. You learn the art of waiting. Each spasm of pain or thundering heart or cramped muscle has its own span, its own rhythm, and you learn to wait until it is done. A part of you counts the beats of your body, and another part of you keeps walking, keeps talking, lifts the shoulders and shortens the stride and makes you move forward. You move through the pain, knowing that it will end. Knowing, at the same time, that this illness is your companion and will greet you again soon.

## Stirring σ

Tom has been away for work and his friend has decided to look out for me. Hermann takes me to a theatre one night. We watch the performers career across the stage like kamikaze and the words make no sense but in the final scene the back of the stage falls away and the skyline of Shinjuku, its mad burning neon face, is revealed to us like an epiphany. Afterwards we run to the nearest café and eat and drink and joke and at the end of the night, as we are walking to the last train, always the last train, he pulls me to him and kisses me on the lips.

*Come with me,* Hermann says. *Come now, quickly. I'll make love to you, any way you like. I'll do anything you like.* He kisses me again and his tongue creeps between my lips and his left hand cups my breast while his right hand pulls me closer. I push him away and look at his face.

*But Tom is back tomorrow,* I say. *What are you doing? And you have a wife.*

*I know,* he says. *That's why we have to go tonight. To a hotel. A park. Anywhere. Come on.*

I feel the wine running through my veins and his cock against my belly as he presses into me again and his mouth writing messages on the skin of my throat and for a moment I consider going with him. Even though he is nothing special, just Hermann, Tom's friend. Then I pull away from him. φ

---

σ  *Come on, you either did it with him or you didn't,* I hear you say to me. *I won't tell,* you mock-whisper and nudge me in the ribs.

φ  But sometimes just feeling the sensation is enough to let you know you are still alive. Without the act.

## Distance runners

We have been given tickets to an athletics competition. World stars have come to Japan and we sit in plastic moulded seats attached to a long steel bar watching as the competitors run and throw and leap on the field below us. The sun is strong and we are very high up in the stand. Below us, the field lies in the bottom of the bowl created by the stands. The surface of the field is dull red, painted with white lines. Circles within circles, long tracks of lines, tiny triangles. Like writing we can't understand.

Tom hands me the binoculars. I know I am supposed to be looking at the other end of the field, but I focus the binoculars on the faces of the competitors nearest us. There is a long jump just below where we sit. Competitors are sitting and stretching on the red surface and I can see that they are frowning with concentration, moving their lips in some mantra, focusing all of their thought and mind on this one task. One girl has bandages taped tightly around her left leg right up to her knee. A cheer goes up and immediately the girl in my sights lifts her head like a wolf sniffing the wind.

*Did you see that jump?* Tom laughs. *Amazing.* He puts his hand on my thigh and squeezes, then looks down and frowns, just like the competitors on the field. *You're getting thin*, he says as though he is talking to himself.

*I'm going to get a lot thinner*, I answer.

Tom swings his head away from me and breathes in deeply through his nose. I go back to watching the field. Around the outside of the field is the running track with its white lines to designate running lanes. In the sprints, the runners can only run inside their defined lane. But the long-distance runners are different. The distance runners start in different lanes, then race for the inside lane of the track. Later on, when they leave the stadium, they scatter across the road, then bunch up, then scatter again like a flock of birds wheeling around the sky.

*Where are the marathon runners?* I ask Tom. *Aren't they supposed to be finishing now?*

He shrugs. He glances down at my thigh occasionally as if he is still shocked by what he has seen. My thin thighs. My bony knees. My wrists like swollen wooden joints. Sometimes I can hear my heart beating against my ribs, knocking up against the cage like an unhinged door in the wind. Tom puts his arm around me and cups my left shoulder with his hand. I sense him exploring bone structure, gently tracing the knobby bones through my fragile skin and flesh.

*I see them*, I tell him.

The runners have appeared on the big screen at the other end of the stadium. They're turning off the road and heading into the tunnel that leads to the stadium. Soon they appear at the mouth of the tunnel. Their thin bodies are strained and the sinews and muscles flex and tremble with each step. Their faces are haggard. Three men stagger along the track, heading for the finish line. Two are close together and the third man is making a heroic effort so that by the time they reach the hundred-metre mark they are three abreast.

Tom gives me a quick kiss on the cheek, then lets go of my shoulder and stands up to watch the distance runners through the binoculars. His armpits are soaked with sweat, even though he is only a spectator. I look around, take in the scene, mark this point in time as another moment that I will be sure to remember. o

---

o  I once heard a marathon runner talking about how he stayed the distance. He said he studied the route and made marker points for himself. This place or statue or checkpoint meant he had got so far, had so far left to go. He buoyed himself up with checks on his own physical state. Legs aching but no cramps. Not dehydrated. I can imagine you asking me about that. *Have you made preparations?* you would ask me. I might feel like crying then. I might tell you I want to talk it all out. My whole life.

# The President's Bodyguard

## *Alejandra Martinez*

I have just resigned from my job. I am standing outside the building. All my work colleagues, or now ex-colleagues, are inside. I no longer have to go in there every day at 9.00, eat my microwaved lunch at 12.00 and leave at 5.00. I am free! I am waiting for Joaquin to pick me up.

I feel ecstatic.

I see the blue kombi coming. Joaquin stops and we beam at each other. Our faces acknowledge the release we both feel. I get in the van.

I kiss him passionately.

'Congratulations,' he says. 'Welcome to the life of the poor but free.'

The word poor slightly unnerves me. Did I do the right thing? Of course I did. I don't have children, I'm thirty-four, if I don't decide to do this now I never will.

'Let's go and get something to eat,' Joaquin says.

We stop the kombi outside a small Lebanese restaurant nearby. It is empty except for one table where an old man is sitting, holding his beads in his hands, drinking coffee. A bald man is sitting opposite him.

The tables are covered with white tablecloths, places set,

waiting for customers. The walls have posters of Lebanon, the type you get from travel agencies.

We choose a table by the window and sit down. The bald man gets up from his table and comes over to us. He gives us the menu and stands over us while we look at it.

'We need more time,' I say.

'Of course, no problem.' He goes back to his seat and says a few words in Arabic to the old man.

'What are you going to have?' I ask Joaquin.

'A mixed plate.'

'Vegetarian?' I ask him.

'No, "carne", meat,' he says.

What a stupid question, I think. Joaquin comes from Uruguay, the land of barbecues. In Uruguay they barbecue everything from the bulls' testicles to the cows' cheeks.

'I'll have a vegetarian mixed plate.'

We call the bald man over and we order.

'Vegetarian only hummus, babaghanoush, tabouli and falafel, no meat,' he tells me.

'Yes, that's OK.'

'OK,' he says to me, surprised. I wonder if he informs all his customers that a vegetarian mixed plate has no meat.

'You like drink?'

'A mineral water,' I say.

'A Fanta,' Joaquin says.

Joaquin goes outside to have a cigarette. I watch him smoke. I wish he would give it up.

He says it's too difficult. He has been smoking since he was fifteen. And playing music.

Two workmen come in. 'How are you, mates?' the bald man greets them. There is a familiarity, they have been here before. They order kebabs and Cokes.

Not so long ago, these same workmen would have ordered meat pies and Cokes.

The merging of palates.

Why is it easier to accept a kebab than it is to accept an Arab? Probably for the same reason that we have Chinese restaurants in every Australian country town and we still can't accept we are part of Asia.

I watch Joaquin smoking outside. I want to be more like him. He does what he loves. He doesn't worry about not having a lot of material possessions. Maybe after what he has been through he has developed a skill for filtering what really counts in life.

He learnt to play the drums with his father. Joaquin would play with his father and his two brothers every weekend. Friends of his father's would come to the house and play music. Guitarists, drummers, trumpet players, poets. It was a kind of men's bohemian hangout. They played music and talked politics. His mother and his sister were in the kitchen cooking for the father, the boys and whoever else was there.

Sometimes someone would bring meat and they would have a barbecue, where all the various bits of the cow would be smoked then eaten.

During the hot month of February when Carnivale was on, they took to the streets with their drums, taking their place among the hundreds of men drumming through the city streets. His sister danced in a bikini, with the other 'vedettes', as they were called.

It was a good life, until the dictatorship. So Joaquin came to Australia.

He comes back in. He stinks of cigarette.

The bald man comes over with our plates.

'Enjoy,' he says.

'I don't think it's very fresh,' I say, tasting a falafel.

'It's good,' Joaquin says, 'don't complain.' He thinks that I complain too much. I think I am just stating a fact, he thinks it is a complaint. It is true the food is not that fresh. I have tasted good Lebanese food and this is not.

An old man looks at us through the window. He is pushing a baby pram full of plastic bags. He is unshaven and dirty. He presses his face against the window and begins to show us the gymnastic skills of his tongue.

The old man at the table shouts something and the bald man comes out of the kitchen.

He beckons to the old man at the window to go away, making shooing actions with his hand.

The old man finally puts his tongue away and leaves. He sticks his finger up at the three of us.

'He is sick,' I say, to provide some sort of explanation for the man's behaviour.

'No, he not sick, he bad man,' the bald man says. 'I try to help him before. I open the toilet for him to use and wash.'

I don't really want to picture the old man in the toilet while I am putting a piece of falafel in my mouth.

'You know what he did? He put all the toilet paper in the toilet. He block toilet. It took me four hours to clean,' he says, holding up four fingers. 'He very bad man.'

He walks off shaking his head.

I don't feel like eating anymore. The image of the old man on the toilet has put me off my food.

Joaquin finishes everything off. I guess it's a leftover response from not having enough to eat when he was in Uruguay. My mother does that too. As a child she lived in the country in Uruguay. Her family was very poor. They often went hungry. Now she can't bear to see food wasted. If you are eating a chicken leg and there's some meat still on it, she'll just whisk it off your plate and strip it bare with her teeth.

'Do you think I did the right thing to leave my job?' I ask

Joaquin. It hasn't even been twenty-four hours and I need reassurance. Suddenly I get flashes of debt collectors coming to our door and me as a twelve-year-old having to explain that my parents didn't have the money and they would pay when they could. My mum standing behind me, saying in Spanish, 'Tell him next week.' I knew the debt collector didn't believe us.

'Of course you did,' Joaquin says as he takes my hand. 'You've been working since you were fifteen, it will be good to have some time to write, do what you enjoy.'
　'You're right.'

When we finish, the bald man comes to take our plates.
　'You like?'
　'Excellent,' Joaquin says.
　'Very good,' I lie.

'Where are you from?' the bald man asks Joaquin.
　'Uruguay.'
　'Very good soccer,' he says.
　Whenever Joaquin tells people that he's from Uruguay, the ones that know where Uruguay is, say 'good soccer' and the ones that don't, ask if it is in Africa. Maybe it is because he is black. Those that are more intellectual have mentioned the Australians that went there to set up a utopian community. We know they mean Paraguay.

'Where are you from?' Joaquin asks the bald man.
　'Lebanon. I show you my village.' He goes over to the counter and comes back with a magazine. It looks like a travel magazine.
　He flicks to a page, gives it to Joaquin and says, 'My village.' He stands proudly while Joaquin looks at the picture of his village.
　I don't understand pride or patriotism about where you come from. Maybe that's because I was never in Uruguay long

enough to develop patriotism and have been too long in Australia without fitting in to develop it here.

'Very nice,' Joaquin says. The picture is of a village nestled among a green valley with a huge white statue of Christ on a mountain top.

'Christian?' Joaquin asks.

'Yes,' says the bald man proudly. Maybe he wanted to show us this, so that we would know he wasn't a Muslim. He wasn't part of the terrorist threat. We don't tell him we are atheists.

'How long you in Australia?' Joaquin asks him. They are now both speaking in telegram English.

'Five years. You?'

'Ten years,' Joaquin replies.

It seems as though they are comparing jail terms.

'You like it?' the bald man asks him.

'Yes, I have wife,' he says pointing to me, 'and job.'

'Me no,' says the man. 'Here work, work, work. No time for friends, family. Me here seven days, twelve hours every day.'

'Yes,' Joaquin says. I don't know why he agrees with him. When he really works about three days a week, playing music that he loves. He has heaps of time to see family and friends.

Joaquin flicks through the magazine. He points to a man.

'The president?'

'My cousin,' the man says.

'Aah, you lot of money in Lebanon,' Joaquin says, 'president your cousin.'

'He president eighteen days then he killed. A bomb. Me his bodyguard.'

He pulls up his trouser leg to show us an injury on his calf. 'Bomb,' he says again, pointing to his injury.

Joaquin shakes his head. His face becomes sullen. I wonder if he is thinking about his own political imprisonment.

There is an understanding between the two men. A kind of immigrant men's solidarity.

'I get you coffee and baklava,' the president's bodyguard says.

# Happy New Year

## *Bridget Brooklyn*

The year was just a few hours old, but the night was showing signs of age. Hairdos so carefully constructed a few hours earlier – crowning the blushed cheeks, the lipsticked lips – were starting to topple. Damp strands fell into corners of mouths smudgy with the kisses they had planted on every cheek within reach. Tendrils clung to clammy skin. Parcels of jiggling flesh strained their slithery wrappings.

But the room still had its glow: so much goodwill and so many hopeful thoughts gathered together to slough off the old year. The bonhomie of the partygoers, spreading their arms in welcome to the newly arrived year, gave them a transcendent aura as they greeted each other at the bar with its moonlike luminescence of glass-covered refrigerators. These arms bestowed a fuzzy benediction of flailing hugs on any human shape that entered their arc.

Only the black-and-white barmaid, who had dispensed drinks all night with a nurse's methodical friendliness, didn't fit. The man at the bar with the droopy moustache and droopy eyes had long since abandoned his half-hearted attempts to flirt with her. He had lapsed into wordlessness broken by odd forays into conversation with her, with me, with anyone who hugged him into their orbit on their way to refill a drink. His face became animated when he smiled or joked his responses, as if he felt blessed by the attention. And now even he seemed effulgent as he ventured from his end of the counter to offer me another drink.

\* \* \*

Richard's voice through the telephone had sounded injured, but he had wanted to wish me a happy new year. Happy New Year. Happy Uninjured Year. Anyone else would have rung to send the tight little knot of his unhappiness down the phone line, to sound abandoned and used up like the old year. Richard did it from that core of goodwill which had helped carry us through the worst of the past twelve months with some dignity. But also to keep me up to date on his progress – yes, and to remind me gently that the need for goodwill had not abated, despite this new-found expanse of separateness. And to tell me that he had had some time to think. He wondered if I could find some time to talk. His speech was rhythmic in its almost-planned way: he had had some time to think. Could we meet some time, to talk?

\* \* \*

Someone had kicked the jukebox back to life. Some time to think, some time to talk. The cheap music and the cheap booze were running away with the words.

'Why not have one more, for the road?'

'Why not?' I could never think of a reason why not. One more (why not?) for the road. But why did it have to be for the road? Why not just one more? Full stop. He seemed to find this funny.

Some of the others had drifted off to all-night cafés or other bars or other parties. But there were enough of them left to make it all right to stay perched here, gently swaying, while the droopy man drank with the concentration of his life depending on it. At this rate, I could even spin it out and have more than one more for the road. For the road. Hey, it was another song! For the road, for the road, for the road, road, road.

The rest of the room was still loud; a silence had wrapped itself around the two of us, perforated by the regular *clud* of our glasses on the bar. I wondered whether I should say anything, or whether I should want to say anything. Out of the corner of my eye I noticed him raise his glass and spill some of his wine as he did so, surreptitiously wiping the bar with his sleeve. Perhaps he didn't want me to think he had had too much to drink. He was wiping away his clumsiness, so he could hide it from witnesses who might use it against him. Because anyone could store that gesture away and keep it for later. But I had seen it.

*(If I could get down off this perch – get down, that is, without falling off, I would go to the toilet. To do that I would have to climb off the bar stool with great care. I would have to gather the full volume of my black taffeta and netting around me as I stepped down, to avoid the spikes of my heels getting caught. Once I touched ground, I would have to make sure that the whole process wasn't undone by the very small surface area of my heels coming to grief on the glazed sheen of the tiled floor.)*

My elbow jolted my glass of champagne and sent a frenzy of spangled bubbles sprawling across the bar. No, I didn't want another. Forget about it. I was just off to the loo (to splash my face). I tried again to climb down. This time the stool teetered but eventually righted itself. All I had to concentrate on now was the long walk to the Ladies'.

The graffiti on the walls looked profound. And full of shared femaleness. 'Don't periods suck the big one!' And youthful with the anguish I used to release onto terrazzo walls when no other outlet seemed possible. The raw words ('Fuckwits!') were like the thoughts shouted from the jukebox and pounding through the wall. Pop songs were profound. Toilets were profound. My life flashed before my eyes in jingles and scraps of thoughts scrawled in black marker pen. Some time to think, some time to talk. Some time to think, some time to talk.

In my best moments that evening I had thought myself a goddess in black taffeta and red lipstick. I had turned rather puffy in this clinical light. There might even be grey hairs showing. As I studied the mirror the door pushed open and I clothed my thoughts hurriedly. Then an added defence, my reflected face mimicking girly confidences: 'God, getting older sucks the big one!'

*(Brown kohl over bleared eyes. A sidelong glance in the full-length mirror on my way out, wishing my legs were better. And, heaving the door open, a random thought: I wish I had had children.)*

He was still there, at the far end of the emptying room, bending his elbow mechanically. The remaining partygoers had dug in and were shouting along with the jukebox. A couple of them blew smudgy kisses at me. I smiled, beatifically. I was above it all, could see everything from on high, making my way expertly across the tiles in my high, high heels.

One more for the road, one more for the road, one more for the road. I chanted in time with the jukebox, with the click-clack of my heels, with the pounding of the blood in my head. Above it all, so far above I could even look down on myself as I clacked across the tiles. And on him with his glass of red.

# Fortune

## *Jaimee Edwards*

The first time Josephine woke up it was to the sound of a ring-ing telephone splintering the night. She heard her mother get up. There were clumsy sounds then silence. She listened. The blood in her ears was warm. She heard a faint rushing but not her mother's voice. She did not get up even though she knew that a call that comes in the dark only ever brings bad news. She fell back to sleep.

The second time Josephine woke up it was to the sound of her mother crying. Now her room was light. She got up and went downstairs to find her mother in the living room, on the floor, a soggy puddle of misery.

'Mummy is dead,' she said and her weeping turned into a loose ululation. Josephine did not know what she was sup-posed to do. She felt nothing other than that her mother was far too old to call her mother 'mummy'. In her eleven years she had never known anyone to die. She wondered if she would have time off school. This was not voiced, yet her mother stopped mid-tear and looked up at Josephine in mild shock. Josephine was pinned under her mother's gaze. Exposed. They stayed like that. Then she put her hand on her mother's cheek. To her relief tears slipped from her eyes again. She began speaking. She should not have bothered. Josephine may not have known death but she understood it. She knew that the death formed the light and created the darkness. There was no need for explanations. Still, her mother's white lips parted and Josephine watched her thick tongue move about inside as details tumbled off it.

Her house became the centre of mourning. Josephine's mother and grandmother had been especially close. All eight of her mother's sisters arrived. They were a mass of sixteen arms and sixteen legs. They lived together and they moved together. Occasionally a single aunty would break away, act independently, then morph back into her sisters. Josephine's mother, the ninth daughter, was the only one who did not belong to this multi-headed beast. She had had a daughter of her own, a decision only her own mother understood. But now that she was gone, her sisters drew in close to claim their own. Shoulder to shoulder they stood like a phalanx, impossible to battle. So when they held her at arm's length, scrutinised her blank face and announced she was in shock, Josephine did not tell them the truth. Shock? The shock was their own. Josephine's grandmother had been an old woman with advanced breast cancer. Why wouldn't she die?

Josephine went upstairs to grow up. Hopefully she would re-appear when everyone was gone and she was already a woman.

Standing at the long rectangular mirror fixed to the inside of her wardrobe, Josephine stared at her reflection. It was company, the only thing she enjoyed looking at in the confines of her pre-adolescence. She undressed. Her torso was straight and tight. Her skin, spilt milk. She looked for change. Hope. And there ... there was change, but not the kind she expected. Under her nipples two inflammations had appeared. One on each side. Insect bites. Festering blooms. She scratched them though they did not itch. Strange. There was a dull ache. She went to lie on her bed and ran her fingers back and forth over them. She thought of other things: her orphaned mother and aunties, tumours trapped inside conquered bodies, her grandmother dying. What had it been like? Was it like lying on your bed with nothing happening, nothing in your heart? If so it wasn't so bad.

For days her mother and aunties suffered, keeping Josephine out of focus. The rising damp from their tears made the wallpaper peel. All the windows and doors were left open; to let her grandmother's spirit leave or return Josephine didn't know. Twice the shadows of strange men fell across their door, mistaking superstition for invitation. They got one look at the sad, wet world inside and moved on. Quickly. Josephine watched from the corners. She moved invisibly. Though this spectral state served her well when she discovered that those strange bites on her chest were unmistakably nipples and the skin around them had swollen into breasts. When had this happened? Overnight, over the hours? It had just happened. These ectozoons had been growing under her dirty clothes. Since her grandmother's death no one had told her to bathe or change. It wasn't until she felt an unfamiliar rubbing and something like pleasure did she stand again naked in front of the mirror. They looked like decayed fruit. Sad and wrinkled. Josephine poked them and squeezed the nipple expecting an oozing substance to drain out. Nothing. She checked the rest of her body for freakish change. Nothing. Familiar little hairs and her own nipples still fixed flat on her chest. This was no trick. All was as it had been except for those breasts. Those breasts. In the mirror Josephine faced them. She thought for a moment that she had travelled into an alternate reality. Some slippery other life. She had not. Perhaps things like this do happen, who can say? This however she could say, they were not hers. No, Josephine quickly recognised them as her grandmother's octogenarian breasts hanging off her skinny frame.

Josephine considered the possibility that her grandmother's breasts were there to stay. Not only that, she could feel them grow. Another child may have feared they were being punished for some naughty behaviour. Josephine had no such worries. She was responsible for nothing. She feared nothing. To others her extreme indifference made her either poised or reptilian. To herself she was something else, a fatalist.

The morning of the funeral Josephine woke to find her grandmother's breasts had become engorged to what she remembered to be their full size. Enormous. Silver trails of scarred skin pulled with their weight. They dragged to her waist. She could see straight through to the blue-green veins underneath. She knew her distorted body would not go unnoticed any longer. Since she was not one for explanations she would have to hide them from her family. So she crushed them with a torn sheet wound around her body. She wore a swimming costume on top of that. Then she dressed for the funeral. She had no black clothes of her own and no adult had laid out a suitable outfit. They were in the bathrooms applying globs of waterproof mascara. She went to her mother's bedroom and put on a black satin slip, a man's black shirt, a black woollen vest, black socks and her own yellow sandals. A ridiculous amount of clothes in hot February.

Nobody said a word as they drove to the church in a maxi taxi. Josephine sat next to her mother. Looking at her she realised she had not seen her since the morning of the phone call. While everyone else had aged she looked younger. Younger and smaller. In fact they looked remarkably similar, Josephine thought. She struggled under all the clothes. Her grandmother's breasts were trying to break loose. Her eyes met her Mother's, whose were narrow with suspicion. She was about to speak when they arrived at the church. The taxi stopped and she closed her mouth. Still Josephine blushed in spite of herself.

There was an open coffin at the altar. One of Josephine's aunties gave the eulogy. It was always a surprise to see one standing alone. A dismembered limb. She talked of a time before Josephine was born, sometimes speaking in a language she didn't understand. None of it was of any interest to her. Anyway it was impossible to listen when the atmosphere was like a murderous pillow pressed to your face. Sweat poured from her brow into her eyes. Fortunately it looked like she was crying. When her aunties had finished, her family got up, moving with one body they slithered out of the pew. Josephine sat where she was. This was no act of rebellion. She knew if she got up she would just as soon pass out. Her family turned around, waited, insulted. There was a momentary stand-off until Josephine relented. Really she couldn't be bothered. So she stood up and they parted as she stepped up to her grandmother's body. There she was, pale as ash. She lowered her head to kiss her grandmother but instead put her nose to her cold cheek and breathed in as much death as she could. She held it. Uncontrollably a moment came back to her. Her grandmother was putting a much younger Josephine to bed. The room was cold. There were not enough blankets. So her grandmother brought Josephine a heavy leopard coat and tucked her in. She did not sleep all night, waiting for the pelt's carnivorous spirit. Then it was gone. The moment left, the last memory she would have. With her head still down in the coffin she looked down at her grandmother's chest. There were two lumpy little mounds rising up, unsuccessfully filling the space a double mastectomy made vacant. Josephine itched and burned, her temperature rose to fever, but it was gruesome fascination that unbuttoned her grandmother. She pulled away toilet paper and cotton wool to reveal a flat chest. As flat as Josephine's had been except there was no nipple just an angry pink line. A rushing in her head brought the darkness in. She fainted.

The familiar sounds of crying brought her back. She was surrounded. Her own clothes had been torn open, her attempts at bondage pulled to her waist. Her family kneeled at their mother's breasts. Nine pairs of lips puckered with infant memories. No. Josephine placed a protective arm around the breasts and ran. They followed. A stumbling litter of pups.

She ran through the cemetery. At the stone fence she turned around. Her aunties were not behind her, only her mother. Alone. A very hot wind blew across their arms, fingers, faces, and across the graves. She realised something. It was terrible and true. She saw it behind her eyes. Her inherited body turning against her. Its dead lead weight tearing a hole in time in which all the world could fall through.

# As a Woman Grows Older

## J.M. Coetzee

She is visiting her daughter in Nice, her first visit there in years. Her son will fly out from the United States to spend a few days with them, on the way to some conference or other. It interests her, this confluence of dates. She wonders whether there has not been some collusion, whether the two of them do not have some plan, some proposal to put to her of the kind that children put to a parent when they feel she can no longer look after herself. So obstinate, they will have said to each other: so obstinate, so stubborn, so self-willed – how will we get past that obstinacy of hers except by working together?

They love her, of course, else they would not be cooking up plans for her. Nevertheless, she does feel like one of those Roman aristocrats waiting to be handed the fatal draft, waiting to be told in the most confiding, the most sympathetic of ways that for the general good one should drink it down without a fuss.

Her children are and always have been good, dutiful, as children go. Whether as a mother she has been equally good and dutiful is another matter. But in this life we do not always get what we deserve. Her children will have to wait for another life, another incarnation, if they want the score to be evened.

Her daughter runs an art gallery in Nice. Her daughter is, by now, for all practical purposes French. Her son, with his American wife and American children, will soon, for all practical purposes, be American. So, having flown the nest, they have flown far. One might even think, did one not know better, that they have flown far to get away from her.

Whatever proposal it is they have to put to her, it is sure to be full of ambivalence: love and solicitude on the one hand, brisk heartlessness on the other, and a wish to see the end of her. Well, ambivalence should not disconcert her. She has made a living out of ambivalence. Where would the art of fiction be if there were no double meanings? What would life itself be if there were only heads or tails and nothing in between?

*

'What I find eerie, as I grow older,' she tells her son, 'is that I hear issuing from my lips words I once upon a time used to hear old people say and swore I would never say myself. *What-is-the-world-coming-to* things. For example: no one seems any longer to be aware that the verb "may" has a past tense – what is the world coming to? People walk down the street eating pizza and talking into a telephone – what is the world coming to?'

It is his first day in Nice, her third: a clear, warm June day, the kind of day that brought idle, well-to-do people from England to this stretch of coast in the first place. And behold, here they are, the two of them, strolling down the Promenade des Anglais just as the English did a hundred years ago with their parasols and their boaters, deploring Mr Hardy's latest effort, deploring the Boers.

'*Deplore*,' she says: 'a word one does not hear much nowadays. No one with any sense *deplores*, not unless they want to be a figure of fun. An interdicted word, an interdicted activity. So what is one to do? Does one keep them all pent up, one's deplorations, until one is alone with other old folk and free to spill them?'

'You can deplore to me as much as you like, Mother,' says John, her good and dutiful son. 'I will nod sympathetically and not make fun of you. What else would you like to deplore today besides pizza?'

'It is not pizza that I deplore, pizza is well and good in its place, it is walking and eating and talking all at the same time that I find so rude.'

'I agree, it is rude or at least unrefined. What else?'

'That's enough. What I deplore is in itself of no interest. What is of interest is that I vowed years ago I would never do it, and here I am doing it. Why have I succumbed? I deplore what the world is coming to. I deplore the course of history. From my heart I deplore it. Yet when I listen to myself, what do I hear? I hear my mother deploring the miniskirt, deploring the electric guitar. And I remember my exasperation. "Yes, Mother," I would say, and grind my teeth and pray for her to shut up. And so …'

'And so you think I am grinding my teeth and praying for you to shut up.'

'Yes.'

'I am not. It is perfectly acceptable to deplore what the world is coming to. I deplore it myself, in private.'

'But the detail, John, the detail! It is not just the grand sweep of history that I deplore, it is the detail – bad manners, bad grammar, loudness! It is details like that that exasperate me, and it is the kind of detail that exasperates me that drives me to despair. So unimportant! Do you understand? But of course you do not. You think I am making fun of myself when I am not making fun of myself. It is all serious! Do you understand that it could all be serious?'

'Of course I understand. You express yourself with great clarity.'

'But I do not! I do not! These are just words, and we are all sick of words by now. The only way left to prove you are serious is to do away with yourself. Fall on your sword. Blow your brains out. Yet as soon as I say the words you want to smile. I know. Because I am not serious, not fully serious – I am too old to be serious. Kill yourself at twenty and it is a tragic loss. Kill yourself at forty and it is a sobering comment on the times. But kill yourself at seventy and people say, "What a shame, she must have had cancer."'

'But you have never cared what people say.'

'I have never cared what people say because I have always believed in the word of the future. History will vindicate me – that is what I have told myself. But I am losing faith in history, as history has become today – losing faith in its power to come up with the truth.'

'And what has history become today, Mother? And, while we are about it, may I remark that you have once again manoeuvred me into the position of the straight man or straight boy, a position I do not particularly enjoy.'

'I am sorry, I am sorry. It is from living alone. Most of the time I have to conduct these conversations in my head; it is such a relief to have persons I can play them out with.'

'Interlocutors. Not persons. Interlocutors.'

'Interlocutors I can play them out with.'

'Play them out on.'

'Interlocutors I can play them out on. I am sorry, I will stop. How is Norma?'

'Norma is well. She sends her love. The children are well. What has history become?'

'History has lost her voice. Clio, the one who once upon a time used to strike her lyre and sing of the doings of great men, has become infirm, infirm and frivolous, like the silliest sort of old woman. At least that is what I think part of the time. The rest of the time I think she has been taken prisoner by a gang of thugs who torture her and make her say things she does not mean to say. I can't tell you all the dark thoughts I have about history. It has become an obsession.'

'An obsession. Does that mean you are writing about it?'

'No, not writing. If I could write about history I would be on my way to mastering it. No, all I can do is fume about it, fume and deplore. And deplore myself too. I have become trapped in a cliché, and I no longer believe that history will be able to budge that cliché.'

'What cliché?'

'I do not want to go into it, it is too depressing. The cliché of the stuck record, that has no meaning anymore because there are no gramophone needles or gramophones. The word that echoes back to me from all quarters is "bleak". Her message to the world is unremittingly bleak. What does it mean, bleak? A word that belongs to a winter landscape yet has somehow become attached to me. It is like a little mongrel that trails behind, yapping, and won't be shaken off. I am dogged by it. It will follow me to the grave. It will stand at the lip of the grave, peering in and yapping *bleak, bleak, bleak*!'

'If you are not the bleak one, then who are you, Mother?'

'You know who I am, John.'

'Of course I know. Nevertheless, say it. Say the words.'

'I am the one who used to laugh and no longer does. I am the one who cries.'

\*

Her daughter Helen runs an art gallery in the old city. The gallery is, by all accounts, highly successful. Helen does not own it. She is employed by two Swiss who descend from their lair in Bern twice a year to check the accounts and pocket the takings.

Helen, or Hélène, is younger than John but looks older. Even as a student she had a middle-aged air, with her pencil skirts and owlish glasses and chignon. A type that the French make space for and even respect: the severe, celibate intellectual. Whereas in England Helen would be cast at once as a librarian and a figure of fun.

In fact she has no grounds for thinking Helen celibate. Helen does not speak about her private life, but from John she hears of an affair that has been going on for years with a businessman from Lyon who takes her away for weekends. Who knows, perhaps on her weekends away she blossoms.

It is not particularly seemly to speculate on the sex lives of one's children. Nevertheless she cannot believe that someone who devotes her life to art, be it only the sale of paintings, can be without fire of her own.

What she had expected was a combined assault: Helen and John sitting her down and putting to her the scheme they had worked out for her salvation. But no, their first evening together passes perfectly pleasantly. The subject is only broached the next day, in Helen's car, as the two of them drive north into the Basses-Alpes en route to a luncheon spot Helen has chosen, leaving John behind to work on his paper for the conference.

'How would you like to live here, Mother?' says Helen, out of the blue.

'You mean in the mountains?'

'No, in France. In Nice. There is an apartment in my building that falls vacant in October. You could buy it, or we could buy it together. On the ground floor.'

'You want us to live together, you and I? This is very sudden, my dear. Are you sure you mean it?'

'We would not be living together. You would be perfectly independent. But in an emergency you would have someone to call on.'

'Thank you, dear, but we have perfectly good people in Melbourne trained to deal with old folk and their little emergencies.'

'Please, Mother, let us not play games. You are seventy-two. You have had problems with your heart. You are not always going to be able to look after yourself. If you – '

'Say no more, my dear. I am sure you find the euphemisms as distasteful as I do. I could break a hip, I could become gaga; I could linger on, bedridden, for years: that is the sort of thing we are talking about. Granted such possibilities, the question for me is: Why should I impose on my daughter the burden of caring for me? And the question for you, I presume, is: Will you be able to live with yourself if you do not at least once, in all sincerity, offer me care and protection? Do I put it fairly, our problem, our joint problem?'

'Yes. My proposal is sincere. It is also practicable. I have discussed it with John.'

'Then let us not spoil this beautiful day by getting into a wrangle. You have made your proposal, I have heard it and I promise to think about it. Let us leave it at that. It is very unlikely that I will accept, as you must have guessed. My thoughts are running in quite another direction. There is one thing the old are better at than the young, and that is dying. It behoves the old (what a quaint word!) to die well, to show those who follow what a good death can be. That is the direction of my thinking. I would like to concentrate on making a good death.'

'You could make just as good a death in Nice as in Melbourne.'

'But that is not true, Helen. Think it through and you will see it is not true. Ask me what I mean by a good death.'

'What do you mean by a good death, Mother?'

'A good death is one that takes place far away, where the mortal residue is disposed of by strangers, by people in the death business. A good death is one that you learn of by telegram: *I regret to inform you*, etcetera. What a pity telegrams have gone out of fashion.'

Helen gives an exasperated snort. They drive on in silence. Nice is far behind: down an empty road they swoop into a long valley. Though it is nominally summer the air is cold, as if the sun never touched these depths. She shivers, winds up the window. Like driving into an allegory!

'It is not right to die alone,' says Helen at last, 'with no one to hold your hand. It is antisocial. It is inhuman. It is unloving. Excuse the words, but I mean them. I am offering to hold your hand. To be with you.'

Of the children, Helen has always been the more reserved, the one who kept her mother at more of a distance. Never before has Helen spoken like this. Perhaps the car makes it easier, allowing the driver not to look straight at the person she is addressing. She must remember that about cars.

'That's very kind of you, my dear,' she says. The voice that comes from her throat is unexpectedly low. 'I will not forget it. But would it not feel odd, coming back to France after all these years to die? What will I say to the man at the border when he asks the purpose of my visit, business or pleasure? Or, worse, when he asks how long I plan to stay? *Forever? To the end? Just a brief while?*'

'Say *réunir la famille.* He will understand that. To reunite the family. It happens every day. He won't demand more.'

They eat at an *auberge* called Les Deux Ermites. There must be a story behind the name, but she would prefer not to be told it. If it is a good story it is probably made up anyway. A cold, knifing wind is blowing; they sit behind the protection of glass, looking out on snow-capped peaks. It is early in the season: besides theirs, only two tables are occupied.

'Pretty? Yes, of course it is pretty. A pretty country, a beautiful country, that goes without saying. *La belle France.* But do not forget, Helen, how lucky I have been, what a privileged vocation I have followed. I have been able to move about as I wished most of my life. I have lived, when I have chosen, in the lap of beauty. The question I find myself asking now is, What good has it done me, all this beauty? Is beauty not just another consumable, like wine? One drinks it in, one drinks it down, it gives one a brief, pleasing, heady feeling, but what does it leave behind? The residue of wine is, excuse the word, piss; what is the residue of beauty? What is the good of it? Does beauty make us better people?'

'Before you tell me your answer to the question, Mother, shall I tell you mine? Because I think I know what you are going to say. You are going to say that beauty has done you no good that you can see, that one of these days you are going to find yourself at heaven's gate with your hands empty and a big question mark over your head. It would be entirely in character for you, that is to say for Elizabeth Costello, to say so. And to believe so.

'The answer you will not give – because it would be out of character for Elizabeth Costello – is that what you have produced as a writer not only has a beauty of its own – a limited beauty, granted, it is not poetry, but beauty nevertheless, shapeliness, clarity, economy – but has also changed the lives of others, made them better human beings, or slightly better human beings. It is not just I who say so. Other people say so too, strangers. To me, to my face. Not because what you write contains lessons but because it *is* a lesson.'

'Like the water skater, you mean.'

'I don't know who the water skater is.'

'The water skater or long-legged fly. An insect. The water skater thinks it is just hunting for food, whereas in fact its movements trace on the surface of the pond, over and over, the most beautiful of all words, the name of God. The movements of the pen on the page trace the name of God, as you, watching from a remove, can see but I cannot.'

'Yes, if you like. But more than that. You teach people how to feel. By dint of grace. The grace of the pen as it follows the movements of thought.'

It sounds to her rather old-fashioned, this aesthetic theory that her daughter is expounding, rather Aristotelian. Has Helen worked it out by herself or just read it somewhere? And how does it apply to the art of painting? If the rhythm of the pen is the rhythm of thought, what is the rhythm of the brush? And what of paintings made with a spray-can? How do such paintings teach us to be better people?

She sighs. 'It is sweet of you to say so, Helen, sweet of you to reassure me. Not a life wasted after all. Of course I am not convinced. As you say, if I could be convinced I would not be myself. But that is no consolation. I am not in a happy mood, as you can see. In my present mood, the life I have followed looks misconceived from beginning to end, and not in a particularly interesting way either. If one truly wants to be a better person, it now seems to me, there must be less roundabout ways of getting there than by darkening thousands of pages with prose.'

'Ways such as?'

'Helen, this is not an interesting conversation. Gloomy states of mind do not yield interesting thoughts, at least not in my experience.'

'Must we not talk then?'

'Yes, let us not talk. Let us do something really old-fashioned instead. Let us sit here quietly and listen to the cuckoo.'

For there is indeed a cuckoo calling, from the copse behind the restaurant. If they open the window just a crack the sound comes quite clearly on the wind: a two-note motif, high-low, repeated time after time. *Redolent*, she thinks – Keatsian word – redolent of summertime and summer ease. A nasty bird, but what a singer, what a priest! *Cucu*, the name of God in cuckoo tongue. A world of symbols.

\*

They are doing something they have not done together since the children were children. Sitting on the balcony of Helen's apartment in the suave warmth of the Mediterranean night, they are playing cards. They play three-handed bridge, they play the game they used to call Sevens, called in France Rami, according to Helen/Hélène.

The idea of an evening of cards is Helen's. It seemed an odd idea at first, artificial; but once they are into the swing of it she is pleased. How intuitive of Helen: she would not have suspected Helen of intuitiveness.

What strikes her now is how easily they slip into the card-playing personalities of thirty years ago, personalities she would have thought they had shed forever once they escaped from one another: Helen reckless and scatty, John a trifle dour, a trifle predictable, and herself surprisingly competi-tive, considering that these are her own flesh and blood, con-sidering that the pelican will tear open its breast to feed its young. If they were playing for stakes, she would be sweeping in their money by the veritable armful. What does that say about her? What does it say about all of them? Does it say that character is immutable, intractable; or does it merely say that families, happy families, are held together by a repertoire of games played from behind masks?

'It would seem that my powers have not waned,' she remarks after yet another win. 'Forgive me. How embarrassing.' Which is a lie, of course. She is not embarrassed, not at all. She is triumphant. 'Curious which powers one retains over the years and which one begins to lose.'

The power she retains, the power she is exercising at this moment, is one of visualisation. Without the slightest mental effort she can see the cards in her children's hands, each single one. She can see into their hands; she can see into their hearts.

'Which powers do you feel you are losing, Mother?' asks her son cautiously.

'I am losing,' she says gaily, 'the power of desire.' In for a penny, in for a pound.

'I would not have said desire had power,' responds John gamely, picking up the baton. 'Intensity perhaps. Voltage. But not power, horsepower. Desire may make you want to climb a mountain but it won't get you to the top.'

'What will get you to the top?'

'Energy. Fuel. What you have stored up in preparation.'

'Energy. Do you want to know my theory of energy, the energetics of an old person? Don't get anxious, nothing personal in it to embarrass you, and no metaphysics either, not a drop. As material a theory as can be. Here it is. As we age, every part of the body deteriorates or suffers entropy, down to the very cells. That is what ageing means, from a material point of view. Even in cases when they are still healthy, old cells are touched with the colours of autumn (a metaphor, I concede, but a dash of metaphor here and there does not add up to metaphysics). This goes for the many, many cells of the brain too.

'Just as spring is the season that looks forward to summer, so autumn is the season that looks back. The desires conceived by autumnal brain cells are autumnal desires, nostalgic, layered in memory. They no longer have the heat of summer; what intensity they have is multivalent, complex, turned more toward the past than toward the future.

'There, that is the core of it, my contribution to brain science. What do you think?'

'A contribution, I would say,' says her diplomatic son, 'less to brain science than to philosophy of mind, to the speculative branch of that philosophy. Why not just say that you feel in an autumnal mood and leave it at that?'

'Because if it were just a mood it would change, as moods do. The sun would come out, my mood would grow sunnier. But there are states of the soul deeper than moods. *Nostalgie de la boue*, for instance, is not a mood but a state of being. The question I ask is, Does the *nostalgie* in *nostalgie de la boue* belong to the mind or to the brain? My answer is, The brain. The brain whose origin lies not in the realm of forms but in dirt, in mud, in the primal slime to which, as it runs down, it longs to return. A material longing emanating from the very cells themselves. A death drive deeper than thought.'

It sounds fine, it sounds like exactly what it is, chatter, it does not sound mad at all. But that is not what she is thinking. What she is thinking is: *Who speaks like this to her children, children she may not see again?* What she is also thinking is: *Just the kind of thought that would come to a woman in her autumn. Everything I see, everything I say, is touched with the backward look. What is left for me? I am the one who cries.*

'Is that what you are occupying yourself with nowadays – brain science?' says Helen. 'Is that what you are writing about?'

Strange question; intrusive. Helen never talks to her about her work. Not exactly a taboo subject between them, but off bounds certainly.

'No,' she says. 'I still confine myself to fiction, you will be relieved to hear. I have not yet descended to hawking my opinions around. *The Opinions of Elizabeth Costello*, revised edition.'

'A new novel?'

'Not a novel. Stories. Do you want to hear one of them?'

'Yes, I do. It is a long while since you last told us a story.'

'Very well, a bedtime story. Once upon a time, but our times, not olden times, there is a man, and he travels to a strange city for a job interview. From his hotel room, feeling restless, feeling in the mood for adventure, feeling who knows what, he telephones for a call girl. A girl arrives and spends time with him. He is free with her as he is not free with his wife; he makes certain demands on her.

'The interview next day goes well. He is offered the job and accepts and in due course, in the story, moves to this city. Among the people in his new office, working as a secretary or a clerk or a telephonist, he recognises the same girl, the call girl, and she recognises him.'

'And?'

'And I cannot tell you more.'

'But that is not a story, that is just the groundwork for a story. You have not told a story until you say what happens next.'

'She does not have to be a secretary. The man is offered the job and accepts and moves to this new city and in due course pays a visit to relatives, to a cousin he has not seen since they were children, or a cousin of his wife's. The cousin's daughter walks into the room, and behold, it is the girl from the hotel.'

'Go on. What happens next?'

'It depends. Perhaps nothing more happens. Perhaps it is the kind of story that just stops.'

'Nonsense. It depends on what?'

Now John speaks. 'It depends on what passed between them in the hotel room. Depends on the demands you say he made. Do you spell out, Mother, what demands he made?'

'Yes, I do.'

Now they are silent, all of them. What the man with the new job will do, or what the girl with the sideline in prostitution will do, recedes into insignificance. The real story is out on the balcony, where two middle-aged children face a mother whose capacity to disturb and dismay them is not yet exhausted. *I am the one who cries.*

'Are you going to tell us what those demands were?' asks Helen grimly, since there is nothing else to ask.

It is late but not too late. They are not children, none of them. For good or ill they are all together now in the same leaky boat called life, adrift without saving illusions in a sea of indifferent darkness (what metaphors she comes up with tonight!). Can they learn to live together without eating one another?

'Demands a man can make upon a woman that I would find shocking. But perhaps you would not find them shocking, coming from a different generation. Perhaps the world has sailed on in that respect and left me behind on the shore, deploring. Perhaps that is what turns out to be the nub of the story: that while the man, the senior man, blushes when he faces the girl, to the girl what happened in the hotel room is just part of her trade, part of the way things are, part of life. "Mr Jones … Uncle Harry … How do you do?"'

The two children who are not children anymore exchange glances. *Is that all?* they seem to be saying. *Not much of a story.*

'The girl in the story is very beautiful,' she says. 'A veritable flower. I can reveal that to you. Mr Jones, Uncle Harry, has never involved himself in something like this before, the humiliating of beauty, the bringing down of it. That was not his plan when he made the telephone call. He would not have guessed he had it in him. It became his plan only when the girl herself appeared and he saw she was, as I say, a flower. It seemed an affront to him that all his life he should have missed it, beauty, and would probably miss it from here onward too. *A universe without justice!* he would have cried inwardly, and proceeded from there in his bitter way. Not a nice man, on the whole.'

'I thought, Mother,' says Helen, 'that you had doubts about beauty, about its importance. A sideshow, you called it.'

'Did I?'

'More or less.'

John reaches out and lays a hand on his sister's arm. 'The man in the story,' he says, 'Uncle Harry, Mr Jones – he still believes in beauty. He is under its spell. That is why he hates it and fights against it.'

'Is that what you mean, Mother?' says Helen.

'I don't know what I mean. The story is not written yet. Usually I resist the temptation to talk about stories before they are fully out of the bottle. Now I know why.' Though the night is warm, she shivers lightly. 'I get too much interference.'

'The bottle,' says Helen.

'Never mind.'

'This is not interference,' says Helen. 'From other people it might be interference. But we are with you. Surely you know that.'

*With you?* What nonsense. Children are against their parents, not with them. But this is a special evening in a special week. Very likely they will not come together again, all three of them, not in this life. Perhaps, this once, they should rise above themselves. Perhaps her daughter's words come from the heart, the true heart, not the false one. *We are with you.* And her own impulse to embrace those words – perhaps it comes from the true heart too.

'Then tell me what to say next,' she says.

'Embrace her,' says Helen. 'In front of the whole family let him take the girl in his arms and embrace her. No matter how odd it looks. "Forgive me for what I put you through," let him say. Have him go down on his knees before her. "In you let me worship again the beauty of the world." Or words to that effect.'

'Very Irish Twilight,' she murmurs. 'Very Dostoevskian. I am not sure I have it in my repertoire.'

*

It is John's last day in Nice. Early next morning he will set off for Dubrovnik for his conference, where they will be discussing, it seems, time before the beginning of time, time after the end of time.

'Once upon a time I was just a child who liked peering through a telescope,' he says to her. 'Now I have to refashion myself as a philosopher. As a theologian even. Quite a life-change.'

'And what do you hope to see,' she says, 'when you look through your telescope into time before time?'

'I don't know,' he says. 'God perhaps, who has no dimensions. Hiding.'

'Well, I wish I could see him too. But I do not seem to be able to. Say hello to him from me. Say I will be along one of these days.'

'Mother!'

'I'm sorry. I am sure you know Helen has suggested that I buy an apartment here in Nice. An interesting idea, but I do not think I will take it up. She says you have a proposal of your own to make. Quite heady, all these proposals. Like being courted again. What is it you are proposing?'

'That you come and stay with us in Baltimore. It is a big house, there is plenty of space, we are having another bathroom fitted. The children will love it. It will be good for them to have their grandmother around.'

'They may love it while they are nine and six. They will not love it so much when they are fifteen and twelve and bring friends home and Grandma is shuffling around the kitchen in her slippers, mumbling to herself and clacking her dentures and perhaps not smelling too good. Thank you, John, but no.'

'You do not have to make a decision now. The offer stands. It will always stand.'

'John, I am in no position to preach, coming from an Australia that positively slavers to do its American master's bidding. Nevertheless, bear it in mind that you are inviting me to leave the country where I was born to take up residence in the belly of the Great Satan, and that I might have reservations about doing so.'

He stops, this son of hers, and she stops beside him on the promenade. He seems to be pondering her words, applying to them the amalgam of pudding and jelly in his cranium that was passed on to him as a birth gift forty years ago, whose cells are not tired, not yet, are still vigorous enough to grapple with ideas both big and small, time before time, time after time, and what to do with an ageing parent.

'Come anyway,' he says, 'despite your reservations. Agreed, these are not the best of times, but come anyway. In the spirit of paradox. And, if you will accept the smallest, the gentlest word of admonishment, be wary of grand pronouncements. America is not the Great Satan. Those crazy men in the White House are just a blip in history. They will be thrown out and all will return to normal.'

'So I may deplore but I must not denounce?'

'Righteousness, Mother, that is what I am referring to, the tone and spirit of righteousness. I know it must be tempting, after a lifetime of weighing every word before you write it down, to just let go, be swept up by the spirit; but it leaves a bad taste behind. You must be aware of that.'

'The spirit of righteousness. I will bear in mind what you call it. I will give the matter some thought. You call those men crazy. To me they do not seem crazy at all. On the contrary, they seem all too canny, all too clear-headed. And with world-historical ambitions too. They want to turn the ship of history around, or failing that to sink her. Is that too grand a figure for you? Does it leave a bad taste? As for paradox, the first lesson of paradox, in my experience, is not to rely on paradox. If you rely on paradox, paradox will let you down.'

She takes his arm; in silence they resume their promenade. But all is not well between them. She can feel his stiffness, his irritation. A sulky child, she remembers. It all comes flooding back, the hours it would take to coax him out of one of his sulks. A gloomy boy, son of gloomy parents. How could she dream of taking shelter with him and that tight-lipped, disapproving wife of his?

At least, she thinks, they do not treat me like a fool. At least my children do me that honour.

'Enough of quarrelling,' she says (is she coaxing now? is she pleading?). 'Let us not make ourselves miserable talking about politics. Here we are on the shores of the Mediterranean, the cradle of Old Europe, on a balmy summer evening. Let me simply say, if you and Norma and the children can stand America no more, cannot stand the shame of it, the house in Melbourne is yours, as it has always been. You can come on a visit, you can come as refugees, you can come to *réunir la famille*, as Helen puts it. And now, what do you say we fetch Helen and stroll down to that little restaurant of hers on avenue Gambetta and have a pleasant last meal together?'

# Lore

## *Graeme Kinross-Smith*

'... what does it mean to **me** that it happened ...'
—Judith Wright

*Can I have lived so many autumns, so many afternoons? Afternoons are something like autumns but there are many more of them. Sometimes I think they'll never cease coming, still and warm with the sun, darkening with the wind. Is it possible to have heard so many voices? The mystery trails on ahead of me. I live on in the limpid doubt that I love. Please – no answers. So isn't it strange that Germany shares the sun with Africa, baroque Würzburg in its ice sharing the sun with Chad, with clammy Kinshasa and Monrovia ...*

*How do we reach the inland of ourselves? Minutes pour themselves into a spiral of hours. When and when and when – the seconds pulse. In the photograph her eyes are looking aside to something else as she thinks. The seconds pulse as I take the shot. Then she's caught in the pewter moment of the print. I'll never lose those eyes – hers alone – from the fond theatre I hoard behind my brow ...* bien avant dans les terres ... bien avant ... *There is joy in the happenings that have come to me.*

## SERIOUS JACK

older than me leaning away against the fence after the third
of his strokes he tells me as I am telling you what his father
told him when he was small about Serious Jack whose hut was
on the slopes of Sugarloaf and when they rode up father and
son to see him here was a man unshaven and almost wordless
in a hat like old tree bark who had an eye hanging on his
cheek a wonder to a boy and why was it there on a string of
nerve because he'd tried suicide with saltpetre on a fence
post hoping to blow his head off and lost only the eye that
afterwards he could never afford to tidy up

*The happenings lean down to me ... so many voices, so many of
time's testaments. In books I sometimes read about the passage of
days, days that are gone. Then I write what the voices tell me. It's
like something in reverse, like drawing in the dark, when I write
about the past. Circling me there are the testaments of lifetimes, of
generations – my generation, her generation, the generation of his
mother and her father. Is it a testament when I overhear the voices
of my mother and her sisters talking about their brother Flute losing
the tops of his fingers in the chaff-cutter, hear them saying that that
must have been when his lifetime of swearing began, the doctor back
in St Arnaud setting himself to sew up the stumps with no anaes-
thetic in the light from a frosted window? There are testaments, I'm
sure, to what has been and to what is to come. The voices bring them
to me ...*

## RAYS

... down the far end of that little bay not far west of the head-
land as I dive near to shore my mask will show me the multi-
tude plates of them resting where the sun's warmth springs
back from the bottom in the pale rock basins – one hundred
two hundred babies in a stingray nursery making a repeated
carpet pattern of shovel-nose and tail shovel-nose and tail so
that the retreating wave lets me down too close above them

watching those stings passing below my fins not advisable and further down the bay I'll pass big dark ray wraiths that loom up with their death's-head eyes in the swell, shying away already into the water's blue curtains by the time I see them – curtains of distance in the sea's rooms, or are they curtains of time?

*If I'm putting down words and stories on the computer it must mean that I think there are stories worth saying again – they come from voices I've lost for weeks. There's been no reading, no writing. Now I tap the words in, making a story that I can show to my love. It will be a statement from me and it will say that I have worth, that I am a citizen of the world again. The happenings come to me.*

## OUR FATHER THE BANKER

… what did he wear behind the bank counter in that other time, that other place, behind the wicket gates and grilles, in the humid Sydney days down there in the Bridge's shadow before he came to Melbourne, before he fell in love, before I was born? What did he wear after work, walking through the dimness of Argyle Cut to a game of tennis on the court on Observatory Hill, his mates' voices as they played drifting out like smoke over the Harbour and becoming nothing in the sky? When he later moved to the bank in Melbourne – and to dancing and romance and love and marriage – what was he thinking with his tray during the luncheon break in the bank cafeteria among the suits, the ties, the captured shirt sleeves, the cufflinks, the super-loud tinkling of plates and cutlery? What did he say to the customers as his fingers flashed, counting out the notes, then springing rubber bands round the bundles? One day when we were still boys climbing the white trunk of the silver birch above the quiet street to look out god-like on the suburb there was a hold-up far away beyond the Camberwell hill in the city. A man with a gun leaned close across the counter and ordered my father the banker to hand over a white canvas bag of money. When he came home from the train that night still smelling of the smokers in the dog-boxes our father told us about it. The man grabbed the wads of ten shilling and one pound notes in the bag and ran, but a gun went off and men in impeding pants and coats chased the man down Collins Street. They didn't catch him. Afterwards, the police found a bullet graze on the wall and a bullet dug deep in a telephone book. We felt a thrill in our stomachs. This was our father the banker.

But that is the past …

*… it's like Robert Frost's swinging of birches. It is played out as if only for me. The dew is still on the longer grass along the cow-paddock fence. And it's the wrens and pardalotes doing the swinging – rising on beating wings like pole-vaulters, climbing the air beautifully to settle on the heads of the stalks, twisting to get at the seeds in the grass heads, overbalancing, tipping, riding the thin columns of the grasses to the ground, then coming back for more. Up soar the compact, quick bodies – down go the metronomes of the grasses in a humble bowing to the ground. Grasses, movement across minute after minute in the sunlight – so beat the delicate metronomes of the minutes and the morning …*

## THE GUN

… we stand around the gun. We are young men. That's what the army wants. We are here on the hillside. In the army it's often hot. There are no trees on this hillside. The sun is burning brass above the earth. The earth sings and writhes in its silken mirage. Lying here in camouflage fatigues we can swap places with the sun, look down on this stumped hill-side strewn with men moving on it like blotchy weevils. We can look down and see ourselves. But we are standing around the gun. We know what the army wants. It has to have yelling and slamming shut of metal. It's about obeying orders. It's about being dour and enduring. The army likes detail and ways of survival. Water, ablutions, food, equipment, transport, smokos, lectures, squad drill, communications, dummy runs, swim parades, boredom, maintenance, sentry duty, stripping-down of weapons, leave passes, regulations, boredom and waiting in the dust, mopping up, greasing of parts, bodies lolling in the only shade, boredom and the sudden, beauti-fully inclusive scent of cigarette smoke in the clear, dry air. We can hear the dry caa-ing of crows in the hills. We can hear the far, quiet thunder of guns firing and the brassy crump of shells parting the earth. So we stand ready around the gun, waiting for the orders to come down. Our gun is like a mother. We cluster around it like chickens, doing its bidding. It's big, but not huge as howitzers go. Its khaki sides and bar-rel are slim. Its breech is fat with steel and sweet and heavy like a woman's arse and hips. We have known it a long time, have seen it in all weathers and in many moods. When we first heard it speak, its huge word split our perineums. We reeled, our eyes for a moment seeing only a white wall of shock. Now, when it speaks we all feel a guttural urging like sex in the throat. The breech block flashes back in a blur as the gun utters its tearing consonant and falls back silent. The breech sinks away to its expectant position, like a lip closing over a statement. It sits there, awaiting the tickle of the next shell and the brutal, gasping thrust of Number Two's ramrod. There are just the five of us sweating on the gun, our mother, bringing up her food, making sure she eats it. The gun, our mother ...

But that is the past, my voice whispering ...

*... I carry my grey cogitations about the minutes with me. The hap-penings walk with me. I carry the tone of voice of my story mulling in my head. I find the lane hunched down in its own deep-city dusk that takes a turn where the bins are and the white chef sprawls to smoke for only two minutes on a crate, then gets up to start work again and is swallowed by a doorway that might be a passage to light, that might lead to the nether world ... I will never be able to say all I know about time and where it sits itself and then gets up to leave.*

*I have heard so many voices. I wake from somewhere far inside my
being with things to say, so much to ask. A great, incorruptible hand
pushes the horizon back and back. Sometimes it's treed, there are
copses and breaks, and beyond gleams the untravelled world.
Sometimes it is the dead-straight ruler under the sky of the sea.*

## THE BULL

... I write to my love. I've had conversations, I tell her –
conversations with two huge bulls this morning, one on the
upper side of the road, one on the lower and further down
the valley, both come to the fences to bellow their frustrations
at each other. I had a head-to-head talk with the upper one,
I write to her, where he stood with his white, Hereford forehead curls among the grass heads, looking long at me for
long seconds with his dispassionate eye – an eye that might
despise me. Later when I'm working, I tell her, I see him on
the broad green blanket of the hillside trying to chat up a
heifer. No luck. She keeps shambling ahead of him. Then,
next time I pause and lean on the axe, I see he has another
heifer in his sights. This time it's different, I tell her. It's hard
to believe, I write to my love, how patient the bull is in his
fucking. He feeds with the mooning heifer, nuzzling her
gently. Then he walks with her. His tail switches. He stands
with her, their heads together. Then she moves forward
slowly, a step at a time – and suddenly he mounts her and
fucks her, his thin pistil coming from inside. Then he climbs
down, walks with her again. I tell my love in my letter. He
nuzzles her, explores her hips, then licks her under the chin.
She lays her head back and enjoys it. Then he sucks at his
semen around her tail and levels his head. He's considering,
savouring a scent. He could be praying in a trance. Then she
nuzzles him and smells his penis. The sun beats down, the
grass sings, the two bodies are isolated in the huge green
dimple of the hill. His body is almost twice the size of hers.
They stand beside each other in the deep grass, like two ships
on the ocean. The day goes on, the day goes on in the sun.

The bull and heifer feed slowly on the steady cascade of time, on the further beat of blood the day brings, I say in my letter. I write to her. I know I'm writing down the slopes of a day that will not come again …

*The days sculpt me still in time's elliptical cup. Am I wise? Time and the happenings, like a Japanese scroll stretched between the hands, run through my fingers. I lie down to make love to both sorrow and joy. Even in the present I am in the deep grain of the past and the future runs its silver thread through my navel in this, its one moment, and then goes on shining into light. There are all the pages I must not read, the truths I must not know on pain of death. Even as I look out on this instant's low, probing light I hear footsteps, twigs breaking. It could be time reaching for me. The seasons come, the grass browns, the smells of the earth come out in the dawn and at hot midday and in the damp of early evening. Thousands of years! And this is one day among them – just one. Later tonight the predicted front will come up behind the cliffs in the west. I will hear Gwen's piano notes tinkling down to me from the old house. I will hear the wind's voice change, see the trees stream and bend. I want to be there. I want my days out of all the thousands. I must be there at the ceremonies of the dawn and the sun's retiring below the lip of the sea or behind the cold back of the hill. This is where I am home. I need the grass, the bird calls and wedges of wings in the sky, the sounds of life, the signs of death, the searching of wind in leaves. I need the clouds and the full stretch of the Milky Way snaking from behind the dark of the gum trees in the still black of night. Let this moment print itself on me. I'll adopt the bleak stubbornness of tussocks. No answers. I'll hear the voices. No answers. Just this softly doubting day, and then another and another …*

# Where Here Is

*Graeme Kinross-Smith*

I haven't said all I want to say about time.

The blowflies die and remain in the tracks of the sliding window. I sit close by reading where there is good light. It is here. I read on in this room. People are always photograph-ing each other, the book says. The photographs capture faces smiling. People don't know that each snapshot of a face may tell a lot about the future, as well as about now. There are smiles and smiles, is what the book is saying. Each photo-graph is here. It is now. Just for a fraction of a second – a 60th, or a 125th – and then immediately it is not here, it is not now.

I cannot say all I want to say about time.

Now it is what we call midday. It is still this place. This is where I am. I hear the roof crack in the heat. This is where here is, where I am. Will she come here? Will she find me? I am here. She is there. But she could be here. This is the place that time has reached.

Now it is what we call afternoon, the wind streaming the grass heads, the sun reaching in to the leaves and retreating as the branches move. Last night's thunder and sudden, brief rain scuds have gone. I can hear the door of the rough porch banging dumbly when the wind grabs it. Things are drying out again.

Here she is. Now she too is here. She sits studying her legs on the edge of the small dais. She fills my eyes. I love her contralto voice and her shoulders in the green top leaning down. Outside, the work gloves I used yesterday in the wet when I was splitting the wood are drying on the makeshift clothesline strung between tree branches. I can see the gloves from here, bobbing like unsure hands. Now it is another time. The sun has moved on through the leaves. It is roughly what we call evening, but with the time change that's not quite true – the sun's time is an hour earlier. The sun is still here. Its steady, streaming face masterminds everything I see, every ruck in the rug of the paddocks. I have the feeling that it is not quite now, that it is some other time.

The men died there. They died up the road. It was not quite here, and I'm not sure exactly where the ute left the road and rolled. I'm not sure where their bodies lay, separated from each other in the grass. My neighbour Jack found them. First he saw the ute on its side and went to look. Then he found one man – he bent down gingerly: no breathing, no carotid artery. Then stumbling about and swearing with dread and surprise he found the other man up nearer the road. His clothes were peeled down his body, probably by the seatbelt that had torn apart. Dead – probably trying to haul himself up towards the road. Both of them crushed. What is the difference between the slow-burning brazier and private ballet of life and the ash-cold stillness of death? There was a bottle of whisky in the ute, Jack said – and syringes. Who knows, he said. It was none of my business, if you know what I mean. None of it was here: it was there where the road bends near the top of the hill, near the entrance to the Potter farm. It was then. The time of the men reached a place and then it stopped.

I still haven't said everything I want to say about time or about death after life. But if I die without warning will I want it to be down in the sea's beautiful rooms of flowing tresses or would I like it to be on a hillside in grass with the spangled notes of larks far up against the blue? It would be then and it would be there. It's then, I realise, that I will stop remembering. But at the moment it comes it will be now and here. There will probably be no choice. Just like Jack my neighbour who found the two men, and then two months later was face down himself on the bank of the creek when they found him. Heart. He'd gone down there on the horse to bring up a couple of mavericks to the crush – rain and plenty mud. So when he doesn't come back to the fuggy kitchen and when Gwen his wife has been round the other cattle to check the calves, their neighbour Paul on the other side is coming up the drive. Jack was going to meet me, he says. It was then. It isn't now. It was there, not here. So Paul goes to look – up the top first, near the windmill, and yes, there are three Herefords in the truck but none in the yard. It's still raining in heavy sheets across the face of the hill. He goes down to the creek. He comes back. Gwen asks him, her face lighting. You better not go down there, he says. She sways with sudden worry and turns to get her old oil coat. He stops her. She's quivering. Ring the Doc, he says. And the Doc comes, the smell of rain on his coat in the kitchen. Not long after him the ambulance comes up round the road's bends like a slow turtle from Benton.

Jack always said that when he went he wanted to go in the paddock.

I might never say all I want to say about place and time. What am I supposed to do? There will be many other happenings that will come to sit near me. I will still breathe, watching each quivering movement until the happening is over. I will wait for the light to settle. There may be the dark clouds like enforcers behind the forest at the head of the valley, there may be the sheen of rain on the road. Afterwards, I will probably turn again to the axe – trimming, splitting – and time will step gently around me. The next burst of sun will reach its fingers into the lopped branches where they lie on the ground. It will draw out the sad wine smell of sap that the tree has spent all its life hoarding.

# Notes on Contributors

**Alli Barnard** studied scriptwriting at school and is soon to be published in the Sydney zine *Queer Little Fish*. 'Finding the Way Home' is her first published story.

**Tiffany Barton** is a student at Curtin University in Western Australia. Her story 'The Hammam' won second place in the tertiary section of the 2002 Canberra University National Short Story Competition. This is her first appearance in a major publication. She is currently working on a book of short stories.

**Nathan Besser** is a young writer from Sydney. He also delivers pizzas.

**Bridget Brooklyn** trained as a historian, but is now employed as a shop assistant while working as a singer and actor in Sydney. 'Happy New Year' is her first published story.

**J.M. Coetzee** was awarded the Nobel Prize for Literature in 2003. His work includes the novels *Youth, Disgrace*, which won the Booker Prize, and *Elizabeth Costello*. He was born in Cape Town, South Africa, and is now a resident of Australia. 'As a Woman Grows Older' first appeared in the *New York Review of Books*, 15 January 2004.

**Susan Coleridge** won the short story section of the 2002 Southern Cross Literary Competition with her story 'Unfinished Business'. Her junior fiction novel, *Gold Fever*, which is set on the Ballarat goldfields, will be published by Lothian Books in 2006.

**Jaimee Edwards** was born in Sydney in 1977. As a child she lived in New Zealand, England, the United States and Canada. She studied creative writing at Griffith University on the Gold Coast and RMIT in Melbourne. She currently lives in Katoomba, NSW.

**Delia Falconer** is the author of *The Service of Clouds*. Her second novel, *The Lost Thoughts of Soldiers*, will be published by Picador in 2005.

**Erin Gough**'s short stories have been published in journals including *Southerly*, *Overland* and *Imago*. She was recently granted a Varuna Fellowship, and intends to spend her time at Varuna working on her first novel.

**Steve Holden** is a Melbourne journalist and writer. He is the editor of *Teacher* and *Professional Educator*.

**Graeme Kinross-Smith** is a poet, writer and photographer. He has recently finished writing a literary novel.

**Joanna Kujawa** was born in Poland and has lived in several countries and published in nearly all of them. Presently, she has settled in Melbourne. Her first publication in English was in *Hard House Review* in Canada. 'Dreaming Havana' was first published in *Heat* magazine.

**Kathryn Lomer** has published a novel, *The god in the ink* (2001), a collection of poetry, *Extraction of Arrows* (2003), and a young adult novel, *The Spare Room* (2004), all with University of Queensland Press. She lives in Hobart. 'Class of '73' won the 2004 Glen Eira *My Brother Jack* Short Story Award.

**Rae Luckie**'s passion is helping people to preserve their life stories. Currently teaching part-time at the University of Wollongong, she is a Ph.D candidate in autobiographical writing at the University of Western Sydney.

**Alejandra Martinez** lives in the Blue Mountains, New South Wales, with her partner and three children. She was born in Uruguay and came to Australia when she was seven years old. In 2004 she had her first play performed, *Mi Tango*.

**Rose Michael** is a writer and editor of fiction and non-fiction. Her first novel *The Asking Game*, of which 'end sex' is an extract, was runner-up in the 2002 *Australian*/Vogel Literary Award. She is currently editor of *Australian Bookseller & Publisher* magazine and the *Weekly Book Newsletter*.

**Paul Mitchell** won the 2004 University of Canberra National Short Story Competition. His fiction has appeared in *Overland*, *Island* and the Cardigan Press anthology *Normal Service Will Resume*. His book of poetry, *minorphysics*, was released by Interactive Press in 2003.

**Creed O'Hanlon** is a creative polymath who describes himself as 'living on the fringes of nearly everything'. His writing is featured regularly in the *Griffith Review* and *The Bulletin*.

**i.j. oog** was born in Utrecht in the Netherlands. He emigrated to Australia in 1980 and now lives in Wagga Wagga, New South Wales. He holds a doctorate in fine art.

**Paddy O'Reilly** writes fiction and screenplays. Her stories have won a number of national awards, including *The Age* and the Glen Eira, *My Brother Jack* short story competitions. 'Distance Runner' was the winner of the Judah Waten National Short Story Prize.

**Amra Pajalic** has had short fiction published in *Woman's Day*, *Australian Women's Forum*, *Voiceworks* and *The Big Issue*. She won second prize in the 2004 Short Story Section of the Wildfire Literary Competition with her erotic story 'Eunuch-que Pleasure', and 'Siege' won equal third prize in the 2001 Glen Eira *My Brother Jack* Short Story Award.

**Kay Readdy** is a Melbourne writer who has worked as secretary, sales consultant and teacher of English as a second language.

**Ellen Rodger** has just completed her first novel. Her short stories have appeared in various anthologies and magazines.

**Carla Sari**, born and educated in Italy, has been writing poetry and short fiction since the early 1990s. She has been published in various journals both in Australia and overseas.

**Jena Woodhouse** is the author of the poetry collections *Eros in Landscape* (Jacaranda Press, 1989) and *Passenger on a Ferry* (UQP, 1994), as well as the award-winning children's novella *Metis, the Octopus and the Olive Tree* (UQP, 1994). She is currently working on a Ph.D in creative writing.